THE INJECTED WEAPON

BY PAM FOX

PublishAmerica
Baltimore

First printing

PublishAmerica has allowed this work to remain exactly as the author intended, verbatim, without editorial input.

Hardcover 978-1-4512-7129-4
Softcover 978-1-4512-7130-0
PUBLISHED BY PUBLISHAMERICA, LLLP
www.publishamerica.com
Baltimore

Printed in the United States of America

SPECIAL THANKS TO

MY EDITORJULIE RIVIAD WITH OUT HER
THESE BOOKS WOULDN'T HAVE BEEN POSSIBLE

CHAPTER ONE

Light flickered through the crack of my eyelid revealing a haze of dust floating above me. As my eyes adjusted to the dimness, panic flowed through my body leaving a heavy sense of dread. Looking around the small room, I found myself on a table with my hands and feet bound together tightly. The smell of rotting flesh rose from the floor. I looked down and a body appeared out of a tangled heap of twisted limbs and clothes.

"Matt is that you? Are you okay? "Matt!" I whispered, wondering if he was alive. There was slight movement on the floor as he started to stir. Matt was an average—sized man with brown hair and a body that was lean and tight. He looked as if you could easily take him in a fight, but trust me; he was a lot more dangerous than he appeared. We had entered the Marines together and I knew what he was capable of. He turned and looked at me with a familiar smile that said," what the F…?" as he struggled to lift himself off the floor using the edge of the table.

"Matt, what the hell is going on? Where are we? I whispered as I tried to calm the terror that was causing my heart to speed up. Matt put his finger to his lips to silence me and made a movement to get closer. I waited for him to speak, letting the questions lay cold in my dry throat as I tried to remember what had happened. I couldn't recall anything except being told we had been chosen for a secret mission and were being taken to a place to be briefed. From that point, I remembered nothing. What had happened?

Looking down at my body, dried blood covered my clothes and the table I was strapped to. I started to struggle. I wanted to check myself for injuries but the leather bands held me down keeping me close to the reek of the wet surface. They held tight, my shoulder felt numb and my right arm was useless where it had fallen asleep under my body.

"Matt! Get up here! Get me loose! " I didn't care who heard me. I was getting angry. I pulled hard on the leather straps and they cut deeper into my already tender arms. I didn't like the feeling of helplessness, especially being held down. It was one of the things that got to me, probably a reaction from childhood when I was a lot smaller than my peers. My brother had always thought it was funny to hold me down and watch me lose my cool as I tried to buck him off. From a young age I found that I had to outmaneuver someone that was larger than me, always thinking ahead of what his next move would be.

"It will be okay.

Hold still Julie." I felt Matt lean toward my side and begin working to free the bands that held me. He stopped to stroke my hair, but I wasn't having any of it.

"Stop that! Will you just get me loose!" Matt blew out the breath he was holding and picked up the pace. "I was just trying to comfort you!"

"Just get me loose! I don't need any comfort!"

"Alright you're done. Can you walk?"

I could hear regret in his voice. I swung my legs to the side of the table and as my feet touched the ground, a new strength went through my body. It was odd, like a heat surge. I closed my eyes as I felt the rush. What was that, I thought to myself.

"We have to get out of here," I mumbled. In the back of my mind I knew time was limited and we were in danger, something was wrong with this place but there was no time to think about it now, just time enough to escape. I tried the door and couldn't believe when it opened and we were in the hall. The walls were covered with vines and roots carved out of the damp earth. They gave the impression that we were underground. Light scattered in the distance as we both crept down the damp enclosure, looking for the exit. Doors lined the walls, cut outs in the earth where holding cells once stood. The place looked worn down, some of the old doors were scattered about the floor and we had to watch our step, we moved over the disarray that was in our path. From the looks of the place it hadn't been used in a long time. We moved forward in silence. My heart was pounding so fast I thought someone was going to hear it. Passing a closed door, I heard a full-fledged gasp of pain coming from inside. I looked at Matt and pointed toward the sound. We moved to the door.

Looking inside a shape could be made out. It was the figure of a man chained to the back wall. His shoulders were slumped as his body weight pulled against the chains. His clothes had been discarded and dirt and sweat covered his strong body making the light reflect off of each well-defined muscle. I couldn't help but admire his 6'5" frame and body that resembled a Viking warrior. I held my breath when I saw the amount of blood that covered him and the floor. It looked like he had taken a horrible beating. The blood streaked down the sides of his face and his head was slumped forward in a mass of dark hair. As I watched, the head lifted and gold eyes looked into mine. I froze, thinking he must be close to death; blood flowed from all over his body.

"Come on, we need to get him loose," I said, moving forward to the door, pulling on the heavy weight.

"Julie, I don't know, we really need to get out of here and we can't move him, he's too big." Matt touched my arm and tried to lead me down the hall.

"Look Matt, we can't just leave him here. Are you going to just stand there or are you going to help me?" Annoyed, I wondered what was wrong with him? We were trained not to leave anyone behind, ever.

"He looks dangerous. We could get out and then call someone to come back for him," Matt said, pulling me harder in the other direction.

"We can't just leave him! And you are hurting my arm!" I looked over at the large man with the tired eyes. He was watching us with a strange look on his face. I thought I saw him grin. It quickly disappeared when he saw me looking.

"Okay, we are wasting time." I pulled my arm away from Matt and moved back to the cell door. Reluctantly, Matt followed and helped me lift the heavy metal latch that locked the door from the outside. Inside, the small room was scattered with broken furniture and trash, the man had put up quite a fight. Matt and I went to look at the chains that held the nude man to the wall. They were strong and looked unbreakable, held firmly to the stonewall. I searched the room for the keys and found them on a ring inside the entrance by the door. I tossed them to Matt who started working on the locks while I found what was left of the Viking's clothes. After the Viking was freed and clothed, he moved to the table and gathered what looked like five small syringes and a leather bag of personal effects that had been scattered over the surface of the table. Without a word, the three of us moved into the damp dirt hall, a light could be seen in the distance and we formed a V formation with two of us against the walls, the other up the middle. As stealth as possible, we neared the bright end of the hall; muffled noises could be heard outside. We hid ourselves in the dark shadow spaces around the entrance of the cave-like structure, straining our ears to hear the danger that lay beyond. A radio and muffled men's voices could be heard in the distance.

Rain hung in the air, the heaviness was a blanket on my skin, and it smelled of rotting vegetation as it reached my nose. We had to be close to water, the air was full of humidity and the heat made the sweat roll off our bodies. Standing by the opening with no weapons, I felt an overwhelming sense of danger. I tried to put my fear aside and replace it with anger; it was a method, a practice that had always calmed me. I recited in my mind: I am a Marine. I am a Marine! Matt and I had been trained to use our hands and bodies as weapons, I knew we were forces to be reckoned with. Looking at the Viking, with his large frame and determined look in his eyes, I was glad he was on our side. I must have looked in his direction because there was that grin again. I gave him a mean look but he almost smiled. Just because I was small didn't mean I wasn't powerful! Trust me, I had earned the respect of others and could take care of myself. Many a man had thought because of my 5'5 frame, blond hair and curvy ass, I was a pushover. But they always found out later that my quick reflexes, lean muscular physique and training could take down most men.

Silent as possible, we moved to the opening. Outside there was a small tent 20 feet from where we stood; guns and ammo covered the ground. Inside, four men were sitting at a makeshift table playing some kind of card game, money was piled up in the middle and looked to be getting higher as we watched. The men were wearing dirty military issue clothes, and had grown-out facial hair. They looked like they hadn't bathed in a while. I wondered who had us? The soldiers I knew would never be caught looking as unkempt as these men. As I listened, I thought I was hearing English. What the hell…What was going on? Where were we? An old military flatbed pick-up truck was parked near the tent. It looked dusty, mud covering the tires. A small breeze blew some air through the cave opening and the smell was overpowering. I remembered the scent; I had smelled it before, but couldn't put my finger on it. I looked at Matt and he pointed at the truck. I looked at the Viking; he shook his head and pointed in the direction of the trees. I looked at Matt and pointed to the trees. He didn't look happy but nodded his head. MEN! Testosterone! Slowly, while the guards were preoccupied with their game, we crept into the woods.

******

Washington DC—2 Months Earlier

Checking at the front desk, the packet had arrived. The Commander had been waiting for it the last twelve hours since arriving in town from Eglin Air Force Base in Florida. He was a little stressed; this wasn't like anything that he had been assigned to in the past. He had a meeting with a politician here in Washington, DC, though the orders were turning out to be a little unusual. He had been told to come to the hotel to wait for directions. The military had been his life for over twenty years and he had been stationed all over the world. This is why, he guessed, he had been sent on this strange assignment. All that he had been told was that it was a highly classified and secretive operation. No one was to know where he was going when he left the base in Florida. His orders stated he was to be gone for two weeks, he wondered if he would be in Washington the whole time. He knew the higher—ups regarded him as a man that would do anything for his country because he had proved himself in the past. He never questioned, just did what he was told.

Taking the packet he went to his room to see what was required of him now. Opening the envelope, the orders fell into his hand, along with a new driver's license and credit card. The name Nick Samson stared at him under a picture of himself.

The orders were strange:

Oasis Gardens, Saturday, 10 PM, Table 5,

Bring bottle of Alcohol

Dress Casual

No Weapon Looking at his watch he had two hours to get ready. He showered, dressed and found a taxi down the street from the hotel. When he told the driver the name of the place, he knew where it was. After arriving at the club and paying, the driver gave him a smile and a high five. The Commander shook it off wondering about the drivers in Washington and got out of the car. The parking lot looked sinister, many of the lights were in need of replacements and the ones that were working gave off an eerie yellow glow.

He hurried to the door noticing the expensive cars filling the dark parking spaces. The entrance was not well lit and there was no sign of the name of the club. He walked to the door and stepped into a dark entryway, music could be heard in the distance. A woman in a slinky, tight black dress with enhanced breasts appeared from behind a curtain. She welcomed him and took his bottle of alcohol, pulling it out of the brown paper bag. He was given a ticket with a number on it; he shoved it into his pants pocket. It reminded the Commander of the kind they give you at elegant city clubs where they have coat checks. His driver's license and credit card were taken to copy and he was handed a stack of forms to fill out.

When the paperwork was finished, he was given a laminated membership card. The name of the club was printed on the front with his new name. On the back was a picture of a couple with their bodies intertwined.

He followed Ms. Slinky through curtains that pulled back and opened up into a large room. It was impressive; the middle of the room was a dance floor, a bar with a buffet was off to the side and stocked with wonderful looking food reminding him he hadn't eaten that day. The women led him to the bar where he was told to give the bartender his number and he would make him a drink with the alcohol that he had brought with him. Looking around he saw a lot of attractive people, of many different ages. Some of them were dressed like it was a strip club with all kinds of low cut tops and glass shoes. The others wore normal business attire, lots of dark suits and polished shoes. The tables had dark red velvet tablecloths with numbers on them.

Eyeing table number five, he made a move in that direction, He noticed a gray haired man in an expensive suit sitting alone.

He had on sunglasses and was watching the dance floor. The Commander thought the sunglasses were a little much for the dark bar but then again, all of this was a little bizarre. Feeling out of his element in this new environment, he slid into a seat and moved away the glass of an unfinished drink from in front of him. Before he could speak a word, the man put his hand up motioning him to silence. "I will know you as Nick Samson, it's safer and you will know me as Frank."

"What is this all about?" The Commander moved to shake his hand and was brushed off. He watched as the man fidgeted with his clothes. It was a nervous telltale that alerted the Commander that something wasn't right.

"We can't talk here, follow me, and just do as I do until I tell you we can talk." Frank stood and moved through the club turning his head in the direction of every woman he passed. The Commander followed the gray haired man, watching his behavior, wondering how he had gotten involved in this kind of mess. They moved to a back area of the club and entered a coed locker room. Men and women stood in front of lockers taking off their clothes and putting everything inside.

"Take your clothes off and put on only a towel, lock everything in a locker." He did what he was told and started removing his clothes, folding them for when he returned. In his head, he was thinking of how to get out of here while trying not to show what he was really feeling on his face. What kind of place was this? Being nude made him feel a little defenseless. Wrapping the towel around his toned torso, he followed the gray—haired man with the potbelly. They moved to a red door that was across the hall.

Bouncers stood looking over the people waiting in line to get into the dark areas of the club. The two men were looked over and let pass into a different kind of space.

It looked like the only requirement was that you had to wear a towel to get inside. Within, the lighting was not bright; people were standing around drinking at a bar. Some of the women were wearing just panties, moving their bodies to the faint beat of the music. The halls ran from the main room, where lots of brightly painted doors could be seen from the bar. The Commander followed, watching as

Frank stopped as they passed open doorways revealing people in many different sex acts. The Commander had never been to a place like this; he knew they were out there, but they weren't for him. Passing through rooms, he saw areas with two to four people, some looked like couples that were switching partners. The hall ended in an open area with at least ten beds on the floor, bodies were intertwined, the scent and glow of vanilla candles lit the room, noises could be heard coming from the floor's direction, it was one big sex feast. His mind was racing—what the hell…He liked sex or watching sex but this was work and he was the type that couldn't relax until the work, was done. He had never understood men who went to strip clubs for lunch with clients. He didn't know what this Frank guy had in mind, but he was here to take care of business, not to romp in the sheets. It was hard to act like this was no big deal when most of the people were walking around carefree and nude, their white bodies glowing in the dim light. This place was where some couples came to spice up their love lives. But looking around it seemed it would also be a place to really mess up your relationship. He thought these people were really fooling themselves if they believed their relationship could make it past sleeping with other people.

Frank stopped at a room that no one was in and they moved inside. As the door was shut, panic started to rise, If this mother F…makes a move, I am going to lay him out flat, forget this assignment.

"Nick, sorry to bring you here, but this is the only place I could think of that we could talk without anyone overhearing us." Frank leaned against the wall studying the Commander for the first time. He watched as he made a move to sit on the bed and waved him to stay standing.

"This bed is not clean," Frank said. At that point he tried not to even touch the walls, hands behind his back in an at-ease stance. He looked at the trash; it was full of rubbers and used Kleenex.

"All right, what is with all of this hiding out?" The Commander said, looking around. "What is my assignment?" Frank pulled out the folder from under his arm and opened it.

"No one is to know about this, the government has approved money for military research. Our job is to see that the research is carried out. You are in charge of the people we will use for this project. They are to be delivered to a research area in the backwoods; the place is in the middle of some swampland in Georgia. It has been set up and will be completely hidden from outsiders. You will turn the people in these files over to a scientist named Belvar; he is doing the experiments and the testing. These are the test subjects that you are to pick up. All the information is inside. If you need to reach me, call this number, leave a message and I will get in contact." Frank handed him the folder. He took it and flipped through and saw a blond girl, she was good looking and had innocence about her.

"What's with the girl, she looks normal?" The Commander asked, looking down at the page.

"Don't be fooled, she's anything but normal, she's exceptional" Frank said. The Commander shut the folder and concentrated on getting the hell out of the sex den after he understood his job.

"Now that we are done with business, I will go." Looking down at Frank's fidgeting hand, he reached for his empty glass. "Here, I will take your glass for you." The Commander moved to the door, taking the cocktail glass from Frank's outstretched hand.

"You sure you don't want to stay and hang out a while?"

Here everyone is nameless and you can fulfill any fantasy you want and no one cares." Frank's towel started to slide down as an invitation and by the time the Commander looked back all he could see was his white belly glimmering in the soft light. Politicians—did they always think they could do what they wanted with no consequences? As he left, he didn't notice any of the people that lined the walls and filled the bar, he could only see the face of the young girl in the picture.

CHAPTER TWO

Creeping through the woods, I noticed that the sky had opened up and the rain was coming down hard. At least it would cover our tracks and make us hard to find. My clothes felt heavy; I wanted to discard them but knew I would need them later to survive. Not only was the rain pouring down hard, the water level on the ground made moving with any speed impossible.

Looking at my feet, I saw that I was in about six inches of water and as we moved away from the camp into the swamp, the water level was rising. I couldn't remember when I had last had anything to eat and was surprised that I was still full of energy, I felt strong. The Viking had taken charge and Matt and I were following him. He was at ease in the wilderness as if this happened to him every day. His large frame moved like a big cat and he was quick on his feet. We hadn't had time to talk because we were still in danger. Matt was the one that seemed to be having a hard time, he looked tired and even with the physical exertion, and his body was cold. Hours had gone by and we pushed on. The water had risen to our knees and I was afraid of what might be in the dark liquid. We must have been crossing a river as I could see a large area opening up through the trees. We weren't going to have a lot of cover if we didn't stick to the denseness of the forest. I knew it would get worse before it got better. The sun would be setting soon; this was the last place I wanted to be after dark. The Viking must have been thinking the same thing because he stopped.

"It will be dark soon," I said, looking at the big man, he glanced around the area for a moment looking for shelter.

"We need to get out of the rain and warm up, come on let's find a tree." The area was full of trees; we picked one that looked the largest, its branches thick as they intertwined reaching for the sky in the thick forest.

"Let's gather wood and brush above the water line. We should be able to make an area up in the inside of that tree so we can get out of the rain," he said over his shoulder as he moved through the water in search of dry wood. Matt just nodded and we all started gathering branches, he had turned into a zombie and was clearly having a hard time. An hour went by and we had built a little tree house high above the water line. The area was large and by the time we finished, the three of us could lay down with a roof of branches over our heads that would keep out most of the rain and wind. When the sun went down, cold set in, I could see Matt's teeth shaking.

"We need to get warm," I said, looking at the Viking. Matt just stood there saying nothing, I was getting worried.

"Can we light a fire?" I asked. The Viking shook his head no.

"It's not safe. They are still looking for us and are about two miles back. We have to stay well hidden because they will be looking for us into the night," he said.

"How do you know?" Matt asked weakly.

"I was at that compound for eight days and understand that now we are a risk to them. I'm not totally sure what was happening back there, but I have an idea. You're not the only ones that were brought in, all the others only made it four days and then they died. We were all given some kind of shots. I was beaten almost to death, then given a shot, my body recovered faster than normal." He looked down at his strong arms and flexed, feeling the power.

"Do you know how long we were there? I can't remember how we even got there. I don't remember anything." I started to feel the cold air as I stood still, feeling the coolness blow through my wet pants, making chills run up my body.

"You both were brought in three days ago and put up quite a fight. Two men tried to rape you and were trying to hold you down. You got mad and beat their asses. I could hear one screaming that you broke his nose. I think your friend was made to watch but was knocked out when he tried to help you." I looked at Matt leaning against the tree limb; I could tell he had seen more than he would say. He looked down and crossed his arms as he tried to stay warm. I had worked with him many times in the past and was surprised how he was acting—distant.

There was something wrong. He acted like he wasn't listening, just watching the water swirl around his shoes, not caring about anything.

"We have to get warm," I said looking at Matt. The Viking nodded and motioned for us all to get into our little hideout. He pulled the branches in tight to cover us completely and raised his eyebrows at me.

"Take off your clothes," he said with that little grin of his.

"Bet you say that to all the girls," I said, turning my back. Matt just started getting undressed and didn't react. He was too cold, now he could only go through the motions. So much for jokes! Maybe they would get a kick out of my granny underwear. Not a word, no one said anything. What about laughing in the face of danger? Undressed and in our underwear, I peeked at the Viking through my wet hair. Though I knew he would look good, I wasn't prepared for what I saw. His perfect body was marred with scars, white in contrast to the rest of his tan body. Turning away before I was caught, I looked at Matt who seemed almost colorless and had started shaking, the Viking told him to lie down. We put him in between us, his body toward mine as the Viking wrapped his arms around both of us. As Matt settled down, the shaking stopped. I looked across his head and stared straight into the golden eyes of the Viking. We didn't move, both of us surprised, caught in the moment. I felt my body tremble and told myself it was from the cold. His hand reached over and stroked my hair like I was a kitten. I held my breath, frozen, not wanting to break the connection. He looked away and I closed my eyes. I soon fell into a light sleep. I felt safe.

In the middle of the night, a noise woke me. I looked around and the Viking was gone. About ten feet away, a struggle could be heard, first splashing in the water near by and then a cry rang out. Moving quickly, I jumped from the tree to the water below, it was cold and I felt my body chill as it washed over me. About five feet away was a swamp boat made for the low water. On board was the Viking; he was fighting for his life with two men. Not thinking, I fell into action, unnoticed I moved through the cold water. The boat was rocking with lots of force, causing large waves to flow out in my direction. Two men were on top of the Viking, one of them had a strangle hold on his neck; the other was holding his legs down, trying to push his upper body over the side into the water. I propelled myself out of the shallow water and over the side on to the boat, falling on top of the closest man. I jumped on his back, putting my arms around his throat, putting as much pressure as possible on his neck. He fell back on top of me but I didn't release my hold, gripping tight riding him, l squeezed the life out of him. Time had turned to slow motion as I held on, waiting to make sure that he was dead, I let go and pushed him off of me, trying to catch my breath. Turning my head, ready for what was to come, I watched as the Viking pulled a knife across the other man's throat and then pushed his body over the side. We both sat breathing hard and I started to giggle when I saw my granny panties and bra that were now the color of muddy gray water. A look of concern crossed his face.

"Was it your first kill?" He asked with empathy in his eyes. Putting a hand over my mouth, I stopped the laughter.

"No...not the first, just the strangest, I think I'm lost without my knife. I'm Marine.'" He had a complete look of surprise on his face that he hid quickly behind his wild eyes. Here we just killed two men and we were making small talk.

"Many are thrown off by the way I look, you wouldn't be the first. I was the only woman in my class; I had to be better than many of the men. It wasn't easy. I'm sort of like a secret agent but they don't call me that, they just send me out on assignment," I said as I thought that maybe I was overstating it a little. I had only been sent to try to get information about scientists that were working for the government, I was to make sure secrets were safe and not being sold to the highest bidder. Anyhow, I didn't have to sleep with them to get information, just be real friendly. I wasn't going to tell him that, he would think I was just a silly girl and for some reason it was important to me what he thought of me.

"Well it looks like we have a lot in common. Come on, help me get rid of these bodies and let's get out of here, I don't know how long your friend can take it," he said.

The Viking laid Matt on the bottom of the boat; he was still weak, even after the few Mars bars I had found in the side compartment. I didn't understand what was the problem.

The Viking and I were the ones that were the most beat up and yet after a few hours both of us had been fine. Then it hit me, didn't the Viking say that people that had been given those shots had lasted four days. This was the fourth day! Why were the Viking and I okay, really better than okay, while the other soldiers given the shots had died. I needed to hurry to get Matt some help or he might die. What was in those shots? Who was using us as test subjects? Was it the government? I was sure many soldiers would have signed up for the testing if they had just been asked. Most of the solders would have done it for the love of America or at least so they wouldn't have to do another tour out of country.

I was mad because I hadn't been asked. I was a person that didn't like any kinds of drugs in my body. If I had wanted to be a user, it wouldn't have been hard to find anything I wanted at the gym. This was BS and I needed to know right now, I shook Matt awake.

"Matt, do you remember how we got here? What was the mission?" His eyes opened a crack as he looked up at me. "I just remember going to get our assignment and then nothing," I said, watching him closely and trying to read his face.

"Julie, if something happens to me, take this key, it opens a safety deposit box at Chase Bank in South Beach Florida," he whispered, grabbing his chain where the key hung along side his tags.

"Just relax, nothing is going to happen to you! We are going to get you some help. But I really need to know why all this is happening, why me?" I pleaded.

"You never realized how strong of a women you really are," he said reaching and touching my cheek.

"Now let me rest and we will talk later when I wake up." He closed his eyes and I went to the back of the small flat boat and sat next to the Viking. He drove the boat with the ease of an outdoorsman. I needed to understand what was happening and Matt wasn't telling me on purpose. Maybe if I tried to be friendly with the Viking, I could get some information out of him.

"I'm Julie, by the way, we never were introduced," I said, smiling at him. He looked at me like I was crazy.

"I know your name," he said and continued to drive the boat, somewhat ignoring me.

"Well, what I really mean is, I don't know your name or anything about you."

"What do you want to know?" he asked.

There was that stupid grin again I felt my checks get hot, it must have been the sun or he just made me feel silly. I wasn't used to having a hard time talking to men. I grew up with a brother and his friends around all the time. This wasn't working as I had planned.

"To start with, what is your name?" I asked.

"Quinn," he said.

"Quinn, and all along in my head, I have been calling you the VIKING." My head whipped around fast when I heard a deep laugh coming from him, it almost made me jump I was so startled.

"I just thought you looked like a warrior," I said. He stopped laughing and put his hand on mine and gave it a little squeeze.

"That's one of the nicest things anyone has said to me in a long time. I like you too," he said, like he was used to women fawning over him.

"I didn't say I liked you! You're really full of yourself! I could take you down…in the ring!" I spit out the words not thinking. I knew I couldn't ever win fighting this man in combat, but how irritating to think I was after him. A man had not intrigued me in a long time; I was acting silly and saying stupid things like I was in high school. Before he could respond, I was being pushed to the bottom of the boat with such force my breath was knocked out of me.

"Stay down!!" He yelled, forcing me back in place until I felt the medal from the bottom of the boat rubbing the skin off my check. Then I heard it, the power of a motorboat engine and it was coming fast. I must have been in my own world talking to the Viking and not listening, how careless of me to let my guard down. I moved up slowly until I was on top of Matt, protecting his body, covering him with mine. I held on tight. Quinn powered the boat, shots were being fired and they sounded close by, we had to lose them. The noise of their engine was getting louder and the bullets were skimming the water closer and closer to the boat, I knew they were closing in. From down in the bottom of the boat, I realized we had more water then I remembered or it was just that my face was too close to the base of the boat, I struggled to keep my face out of the muddy water as the boat jumped the waves and branches in the murky water.

Quinn yelled, "Hold on." A moment later we were air born, flying over the top of a small piece of land. We flew into a different body of water, landing upright and speeding on through the dirty water. The boat behind us tried to follow and its propeller got caught in the wet muddy bank. The men went flying out over the top of their boat, crashing into the cold water. We continued at top speed in and out of the brush, putting as much distance as possible between our boat and our pursuers. After some time, we turned back into the swamp, our progress slowed but we were out of sight. There was still four hours of daylight and we had to find a place to hide out for the rest of the day. At night, under the cover of darkness we would travel, it was too dangerous now.

Deeper and deeper into the swamp we went, the water level had risen, and splashing noises could be heard all around us. Every few minutes I would catch a glimmer of movement coming from beneath the water and hoped it was just a fish. Finally, we found a small cove that the boat fit into, branches that hid us from the shore surrounded it, and I began to feel some relief.

"Okay what is the plan?" I asked.

"I am going to get some more branches to cover us up and we will rest until it gets dark. Then we get the hell out of here. Can you stay put and not move?" he asked.

"Okay!" I said, a little strong, thinking he really did like to give orders.

When he was out of sight, I moved over to check on Matt, I pushed his shoulder.

"Matt…wake up, we are safe." There was no movement, his eyes were closed and his skin felt cold.

"Alright, get up Marine!" Still nothing. Panic started to rise in me, I moved closer and started checking vitals; my hands were shaking as I felt his neck looking for a pulse. Matt was DEAD. I just sat there, for how long I don't know, I couldn't move. The world had stopped, time stood still. I must have been in a trance like stage because I didn't move until I felt a hand on my cheek wiping away moisture. I hadn't even known that I was crying. Quinn was beside me telling me, "it will be alright." But how could it be all right?

Matt was gone. He had been my friend from the beginning. Quinn moved me to the side and picked up Matt's body and left the boat, walking through the thigh high water. I just sat there and watched as he climbed a tree and covered the body up with branches. Then he was back, covering the boat till we blended into the trees. He laid me on the bottom among the life vests and covered our bodies so both of us were completely hidden. I was pulled into his arms, my head on his chest and I cried, shaking with uncontrollable sobs that I couldn't hold back.

"We can't leave him there. Marines never leave their own behind."

"Don't think about him, he will be safe until we return for him," Quinn said, pulling me tighter against his warm body.

"Here," he handed me Matt's tags and I put them over my head. "Now close your eyes and rest, all will be well," he said. But I knew it would not be all right, someone was going to pay for this, I was going to find the answers if it was the last thing I did. With that, he pulled me tight along his large body. I settled down to rest in his strong arms.

******

As Frank looked down the dim interior of the back of the club, a man came out of the darkness. He was tall with a tan body that looked good for some one in there 40's. His brown hair with its light highlights was combed to the side, a look so many men favored in Washington, D.C. Even in a towel, he gave off the vibe of power just by the way he carried himself. He looked around to see if anyone was paying attention to him before he spoke.

"Frank, you told him your real first name, do you think that was wise?" He said, adjusting his towel, watching the room to see if he was drawing any attention.

"I just thought the closer you stay to the truth, the better it will be if something happens later. I didn't use any last name," Frank stated, a little annoyed at being questioned when it was him putting his neck out there.

"That is why I can't be involved, my name would come up because my office redirected the funds for this project," Mr. Powerful said, as he pushed a strand of hair out of his face, putting it back in place knowing where it belonged to look perfect.

"Are you sure this is what we want to do, shouldn't we start with testing on animals first? This is genetic restructuring and a big deal when it comes to messing with DNA. What if something goes wrong and the public finds out. We would both be in a lot of trouble." Frank turned his head as he watched a nude women come out of one room and go into a different one, her body moving with confidence he didn't feel tonight.

"Look, it is too late to change our minds now, the plan is already in motion. Nothing is going to go wrong, but just in case, we have to be really careful so there isn't fallout. If it ends up working, just think of the control we will have over the military and the President. They will have to do what we say, matter of fact; they will want to do what we say. It is worth the risk. Now how did it go with our officer? He looked a little stiff, but that is to be expected, that is why I chose him," he said, looking around the room waiting to be noticed.

"Senator, he will follow orders, I know the type. Let's just hope we get the results we want," Frank said.

"If we don't, we will just wash it under the rug, no one will know. Now come on, no more talk; I have some women waiting down the hall in the room you like." The senator moved down the hall with a smile on his perfect face.

"Yes, no more talk, the night is young," Frank said, as he followed the Senator, to the softly lit room. Looking from the hall through a window, two young women laid nude across a king size bed. They looked bored as they waited, ideally running their hands over their smooth skin, knowing there was a group that was forming outside the window watching them. Inside the bed was just a mattress and a box spring on the floor covered in a sheet. A few candles were burning, giving the room a glow that illuminated off the tan skin of the ladies. The senator came in and shut the door, dropping his towel and joining the unclothed women on the bed.

Frank dropped his towel, his white skin glowing as he moved to the other side of the bed letting the Senator choose which girl he wanted. It didn't matter how you looked here or how old you were, it was all about the adventure of the night. Sex with the unknown excited him, anything could happen. Here it didn't matter who you were, or what you did, just that you enjoyed the moment. The night had now started as he moved to join the three others on the bed forgetting the project ahead. The door opened and a man came and stood in the corner, touching himself, he wanted a better view of what was going to happen on the bed. Frank looked up and could see a crowd had gathered around the window in the hall, watching them. Soon others would join in the activities on the bed as the night progressed filling the lonely void of the city. ******

Back at the hotel, the desk clerk looked up as the Commander entered the lobby. Walking to the desk he asked, "any messages for Nick Sanson, Room 212?" The desk clerk looked in 212's box and shook his head. The commander was relived that nothing more was waiting for him.

"No sir."

"Could you call my room if anything comes through and would you mind sending me up something to eat and some beer," he asked.

"Sure, no problem Mr. Sanson, how about a steak sandwich?" The desk clerk asked, as he flipped through the hotel's menu.

"That will be fine." The Commander moved through the lobby to his room. Inside he checked the room to see if it was the same as when he left it. Maybe he felt a little paranoid, something wasn't right about this assignment. He felt on edge, his six sense telling him he had to be careful. The food arrived and he sat at the desk and opened the thick folder. It contained twenty files with reports on each candidate. The one on the top was the face that hadn't left his mind, good-looking youthful women with blond hair and a small frame smiled in the photo. He stared at the picture as he started reading her file. Her name was Julie Redford. She was 28 from a small town in Kansas. She had joined up six years ago when her only living relative, her brother, had died in a motorcycle accident. She was the only woman in her group who had made it through basic training. Being a marine wasn't easy and she had earned respect from her unit as time had gone by. After making it through, she didn't stop. She took all the special combat training she could get her hands on. She had some kind of drive that pushed her forward. As he sat there, he wondered what it was that had made her this way; mentally she looked like she was unstoppable. She believed that she was just as good as the men that served with her. Many she had taken down in the practice combat ring.

He laughed to himself at the thought of the small girl besting the men. After reading many of the folders, he began to understand the common thread that connected them. All had excelled in whatever branch of the military they were in. They were all physically conditioned, trained not to fail under extreme pressure. Some were Special Forces, others undercover agents, many were Marines all trained to survive where most wouldn't make it. He almost dropped her folder. How could she be one of them, she looked so cute...so girly? The men she had bested in the ring probably just about died of embarrassment and would not misjudge her again. Maybe he shouldn't care, but what was the government going to be testing on these fine soldiers? The people in the files were at the top of their game. It looked like some of the best. Julie Redford was the only woman. Looking at the photograph, he decided he was going to help her. He believed in following orders but because he had the power, he could make it easier for her. He had seen himself what could happen to women in the military.

He would do his best to protect her. He pulled out his computer and looked up more information on the military database. He found someone who had been with her at basic training and was now in her unit. He hoped they were friends; he was going to contact him. His name was Matt Turner. After talking to him, if it worked out, not only would she get a special assignment, so would he. Taking notes, he planned how and when to pick up all the people on the list and have them delivered. Each would be sent on a special assignment. Before being briefed, they would be knocked out and delivered to the holding lab for testing. This way no one would know where the lab was. He picked up the phone and left a message for Matt Turner to call him.

CHAPTER THREE

We had been meandering through the swamp all night. The passageways were larger, the water deeper. Time seemed to stand still as we moved out of the swamp into a more open waterway. As the sun rose, alligators could be seen on the banks soaking up the sun. I was glad most of our travel had been at night, just seeing them made me jumpy. I found a few more candy bars and some water and handed them to Quinn.

"How are we doing?" I asked.

"It looks like we are coming out of it soon, I have been thinking and as far as I can tell, I would say we are in Georgia." He looked down at his watch.

"Well I was thinking that or South Carolina. We have been heading south right? I said, as I looked at the sun judging the direction.

"As far at I can tell. See that moss on the trees; it is mostly on one side. In the northern hemisphere it is usually on the north side of the trees. At least we know we are in the northern hemisphere, see that swirl of water over there it is churning clock ways. It goes clock ways in the northern hemisphere and counter clock ways in the southern hemisphere, right?" He said with a grin.

"Well I guess it does, you're smarter than you look," I said, laughing, watching him out of the corner of my eye.

"Not really," he said, holding his hand up. "I have a compass with longitude and latitude and elevation on my watch. The elevation has been going down as we moved south, I remembered from some class that I had taken, that taught Florida had an elevation of about only 500 hundred feet above sea level. Teasing me, he gave me a light shove and I rolled into the bottom of the boat, rocking it as I landed. We both sat there and laughed.

"Sorry, don't know my own strength these days." He gave me a hand to help me up. I grabbed it, pulled and he fell down on top of me in the bottom of the boat. Whoops, that was not what I had intended.

"I guess I don't know how strong I am either! I wiggled trying to get out from underneath him. His eyes had turned dark brown and the laughter was gone. We looked at each other; I could smell the outdoors on him; the masculine musk sent endorphins surging through my body. I couldn't move, my heart was racing to the beat of his heart; it felt like a drum was beating on my chest as are bodies pressed together. In that brief moment, a silent connection had been made. I knew we both felt the physical reaction as the heat raced through both of us. Then he was moving and getting off of me. I didn't know whether it was the moment or his 6'5 frame that had taken my breath away. All I knew is that I had a crush! Damn! I hate when that happens, I didn't want to like someone. It makes a girl nervous, giddy and worst of all, weak. It was too distracting in my line of work, you didn't want to care; it was better to feel numb. Attachments to anyone could take your eyes off the ball and get you killed. I had been one of those girls that had a long-term high school boyfriend. He had wanted me to stay in the small town I had lived all my life, get married and have a family. That's what people did in Anderson, Kansas. After five years of being together I did love him, but not enough to stay, I knew there was more out there for me. I was in college when I heard that he had married one of my friends, a fellow cheerleader. Then later that year, my brother had been in an accident on his motorcycle and had passed away. He was all I had left in that town to bring me back. After his death, I never returned. All I loved was gone. One day I was watching TV in my dorm room and saw a commercial about the Marines and wrote down the number and called. Now, here I was. Quinn brought me out of my thoughts.

"Sorry about that." I heard the regret in his voice. It made me wonder if it was regret that he did it or regret that he didn't.

"Hey, no big deal, it would only complicate things," I said, moving a little farther away from him, I still felt the warmth his body had left on mine.

"That's what I was thinking. It would put you in more danger than you are in now. I won't let that happen to me again, no matter what!" He whispered, looking Down as if lost in thought.

"What happened?" I asked softly.

"It is nothing, no big deal."

"Come on tell me."

"Alright, this past year I was working undercover in Brazil. My assignment was to watch a ship that had been moving back and forth between Miami and Rio. We had information that they were transporting guns and selling them to different militant groups in the country, but the guns were never found. We knew something was happening, we thought big loads of cash and drugs were then coming back inside United States through the port of Miami. The problem we had was that we could never catch them with anything on the boat. I was in Brazil watching the ship when a woman left the boat, grabbed a taxi and went into down town Rio. I followed her to an inside parking garage where she went up an elevator. I waited; she came out twenty minutes later and I gave her a head start. She crossed the street and walked to a bench facing the ocean and sat down. There was a long walkway where people were running and walking their dogs. I could see her face clearly; it looked like she was waiting for someone. She turned and looked at me and motioned for me to sit down. I should have known I wouldn't be a good tail in Brazil. I am so big; of course she would spot me. She asked why I was following her and I told her I was interested in buying the vessel I had seen her get off. The next thing I knew we were in bed and she was working for our government bringing me information on the movement of not guns but money to buy drugs. We were together in Brazil and Miami for six months and planning a life together when she was killed and it was all over. Someone had found out that she was working with us and she was gotten rid of. I always wondered how that happened, how they had found out because I was the only one following the trail down there. The only answer was that someone that worked inside our government was also working with them. After she was found dead, I came off the case and did nothing for a few months. It was better when I went back to work; it took my mind off of it. Now it seems so very long ago." He just sat there, staring off into the distance, taken back in time. I moved and sat by him taking him in my arms trying to reach around him to give him comfort, he let me hold him.

"I'm so sorry...What was her name?" I asked.

"Nicole," he said softly.

We sat for a few moments and I just held the big man letting him get it together, he had a soft side under all those ripped muscles. He pulled away, the mood lightened as we both pretended this moment had never happened.

A few hours later we had made it out of the swamp to a delta, the mouth of a small river. We had been following the flow, knowing that all water finds its way to the ocean. Then suddenly, there it was! So vast, so powerful, I almost forgot that we had to keep a low profile. I just wanted to fully absorb the beauty, I never understood how a person could see such splendor and not take a moment. We hugged the coast moving south, we started to see a few small beach homes on the shore with their back decks facing the ocean, basking in sunbeams. Many were deserted homes or rentals that were vacant during the summer months. Most of their business was during the winter when it was cold up north and the snowbirds came down for the sunshine. We moved toward shore, it was time to rest and find some food. As shoreline drew near, I saw a familiar sight I couldn't believe it. A home in the shape of a lighthouse could be seen from the water. It was white and black with a round room and glass windows that sat on top giving a 360" degree view of the ocean.

"You're not going to believe this but I know this place!" Childhood memories warmed my mind as I remembered my brother and I playing in the surf as my parents sat drinking cocktails on the beach. It couldn't be the same place, could it? There couldn't be two houses that looked like that anywhere. Many winters my family had come to Florida to get out of the cold and we had always been on my parents to rent the lighthouse but it was always booked.

"Quinn! See that house over there that looks like a lighthouse. Could you put the boat in as close as you can get it? Over there!" I yelled and pointed over the noise of the waves hitting the beach. Quinn powered the boat through the waves and surf to the shore. As soon as I felt the front hit the sand, I was out of the boat running down the beach.

"HEY WAIT!" He yelled, pulling the boat up out of the water. I couldn't stop myself I had to know. I knew Quinn had to be thinking what's up with this crazy bitch.

It felt good to run, my legs needed to stretch out, being in the boat all that time had made them stiff. The beach was empty. There was not one person on the shore. I slowed down and took off my shoes, feeling the warm sand in between my toes. I ran up the coast, toward the beach houses. Quinn caught up with me and gave me a look, questioning if I was out of my mind. We ran together at the same pace and approached the beach house; it looked the same as I remembered. The closer I got the more certain I was that we were on Amelia Island. The house looked deserted, yes! Rounding the front yard a rental sign with a phone number was posted.

"Alright miss smarty pants, are you going to let me in on what is going on or, are we going to have to find a hospital to check you in?" He asked.

"Okay, I'll calm down. This is Amelia Island in Florida. I'm not sure how we got here, but we must have been more south than we thought. The island is the most southern of the Sea Islands in the chain of Barrier Islands. The islands are on the east coast of the United States. This is Fernandina Beach, my family would vacation here when I was young. This beach house I will never forget, because my brother and I would beg my parents to rent it, but ever year the house was already booked. It is a small island and we need some place to regroup, can we stay here?" I said, waiting for his answer. I sounded a little too excited; I tried to tone down my voice. I could see him thinking, weighing the pros and cons.

"Well I guess it will be as good a place as anywhere. Let's go hide the boat first before we see about renting you your lighthouse," Quinn stated. Before I could stop myself, I was jumping and skipping around like a child in the sand, I looked over and there was that grin. He looked like he was finding the idea of a beach hideaway as good of an idea as I was.

******

Matt's plane landed at Dulles Airport in Washington, DC. He had received a phone call late last night asking him to come and talk to a man named Nick Sanson. He had said he was a military lifer and needed to meet with him about a secret operation that he wanted his help on. It sounded fishy but curiosity got the best of him when the man mentioned Julie Redford. Before he left, he spent some time on the computer trying to find information on the man. There was nothing with the name Nick Sanson anywhere in the system. Matt then thought this might be some old boyfriend of Julie's trying to get the inside scoop on an old romance. The taxi reached the hotel and he took the stairs to the second floor to room 212. Matt knocked on the door; he didn't have to wait long. The door was pushed open to reveal a military-looking man, his stance demanded respect and the look on his face showed he was used to getting it.

"Matt Turner sir," Matt said, as he stepped in the door.

"Ah yes, Nick Sanson, have a seat son." The man moved across the room and motioned to a couple of high-backed chairs with a window view of the city. Nick looked at the lights, admiring what he saw, waiting for the man to speak.

"Well I know you are wondering why I asked you here today. It has come to my attention that you are friends with Julie Redford. Is that true"? He asked.

"Yes we are friends, is there a problem?" Matt said, shifting in the chair. Who was this, her father?

"I am getting ready to send her on a mission, she is the only women. I just need to know if you think she can handle it. I'm from the old school where women were rare in the armed forces. Though times have changed, I just want to be careful," he said, picking up a file and flipping it open.

"Yes sir, she is a good soldier and can handle it just as well as a man," Matt said, tapping his hand on his leg, trying to understand what this was about.

"What about mentally, how is she under pressure? I see that most of her family have passed away," the man asked, watching Matt closely.

"Yes sir, she is stable if that is what you are asking. She is stronger mentally than most, she has more drive or she wouldn't have made it this far," Matt said looking him in the eye, thinking he didn't know she didn't have a family, he wondered what had happened.

"Okay soldier, I just had to ask. I have an assignment for you; it's a little outside the box. Julie is going to get some orders for an assignment. Your assignment is her, you are going to go with her, like you were also sent on the same mission but your job is to keep her alive and make sure nothing happens to her. She is not to know any of this, just that you are working together. Do you understand?" Command was in his voice, and Matt looked at him.

"Yes sir, I can do that. But if you don't mind, can I ask you a question?" Matt looked a little nervous at the idea of questioning authority.

"Yes soldier, what is it?" he said.

"This is a little embarrassing but before I came here today I looked you up and found...you don't exist. I need to know whom I am really working for in case something happens; I'm just trying to be safe. That is why I need to know your real name sir, because what kind of mission is it that a trained soldier would need an escort" Matt said, looking down, afraid of his reaction.

The man looked thoughtful and paused, when he made up his mind he spoke, "Son I understand your concern, these orders are unusual for even me. I am Commander Knocks from Eglin Air Force Base. Here, take my laptop and look me up," he said handing it to him.

As Matt looked up the website for the base, Knocks took out a piece of paper and wrote down some information. Included was his real name and his undercover name. He put a number where he could be reached. As a second thought, he wrote down the club, time, night, table and the contact name of the man he had met. He took the paper and put it in a hotel envelope and sealed it. Matt looked up from the computer as the man handed it to him. At the same time, a photo came up of the Commander and it was him. Matt took the envelope, putting it in his pocket.

"What is this?" Matt asked.

"This is in case something goes wrong and you need help. Put it somewhere safe and don't open it unless you need it. You and Redford will be sent your orders, in a few weeks. Don't tell anyone anything—this meeting didn't happen," Knocks said.

"Yes sir, " Matt rose from the velvet chair and went to the door. Good luck soldier," Knocks said. As the door closed, he was thoughtful; he had done what he could to help the situation. He had never questioned an assignment before; maybe he was just getting old. He needed to know more about the man that have given him his orders, something bothered him and he couldn't let it go. Who was he really and what was the real purpose of the secrecy? If it had been on the up and up, the plan would have come down the chain of command, instead of through a politician. He started writing his orders to send for the people that were on the list. He would have a few days in between each of them to make the plan more organized. The Redford girl and her escort were going to be last, that way most of the testing would almost be over and she wouldn't have to be at the lab longer than necessary. After booking the transportation and faxing out orders, he sat back, the work done.

He pulled out a bottle of liquor and poured more than three fingers in the crystal glass, taking a large swallow he felt a burning sensation numb him. Nothing could stop the plans now; he had followed his orders, done what he had been told, it just didn't feel good. With an uneasy feeling, he tapped into the Oasis Garden's, computer website it wasn't hard to break into the files, the sight wasn't highly protected; it took just a few minutes to get past the security. He punched up the night he was at the club, and found the list of new members with their driver's licenses. There he was, Nick Sanson, photo and all. In the new members list there was no driver's license with a photo of Frank, he should have known this would be a place the man went often. He pulled up just members, there were hundreds of them, this was going to take some time. One by one he studied the photos looking for Frank and tagging the men who resembled politicians. Hours past and finally he found him; he couldn't forget the gray hair and beady eyes anywhere, he finished looking through the rest of the photos. He had pulled out about ten men that looked like potential politicians. Along with Frank, he printed the photos and all the information that the men had filled out when they joined the club. Taking out the glass he had lifted from the club, he rolled the zip lock bag in his hand, looking at Frank's prints. He would run it through the National Crime Information

Center and find out whom he was really dealing with. He might be a person that followed orders, but he always covered his butt in case of fallout. Now he relaxed, feeling the full effect of the alcohol, he stretched out in the chair and fell into a deep slumber. He was flying out in the morning. At his office in Florida he would finish his search.

CHAPTER FOUR

Keys in hand, I opened the door. The lighthouse was better than my childhood expectations. The entrance opened in to a large round room with a kitchen done in white washed wood that looked like the inside of a boat. Big lofty sofas, fluffy as clouds, filled the space. Windows opened up to the beach and the sound of the waves could be heard hitting the sandy shore. I went up the stairs followed by Quinn and found a large round room with sizable windows, in the middle was a huge four-poster king sized bed. We were both stood looking at the bed, oh my.

"We will have to share," I said smiling "It will be better than you taking up all the room on the bottom of the boat." I laughed I was happy; nothing could stop me from being in good mood. He didn't say anything; I could tell he was thinking a little too much and I grabbed his hand pulling him to the stairs, to the room I wanted to see the most. Up we went and then we were standing in the space on the top floor. Windows surrounded the room, you could see far and wide. The ocean went forever, small boats could be seen on the horizon, bouncing on the waves. For a moment in time, looking at the ocean, I felt at peace forgetting we were on the run.

The rental had been easy to lease because it was off-season. We had stopped at a beach house that looked occupied and I had used their phone to call the rental agent, who met us in front of the house. We found that the beach-house came with a small VW Bug and we could use of any dry food goods found in the cupboards. In town when picking up a few things, I noticed that there were some military trucks driving around. At first I thought nothing about it, but they seamed to be looking from one place to another, instead of going anywhere.

"There is no way that they would be looking for us, would they?" I asked, feeling the panic start to rise in my stomach.

"I was thinking the same thing," he said. "Lets get out of sight." Back at the beach house I started cooking while Quinn worked on something that looked like he was preparing to mail.

"What are you doing?" I asked as the fish simmered in the pan, sending the aroma through the kitchen. He looked up, smiled and said nothing. Was he trying to mess with me or did he just not want to tell me. He was amusing, as he tried to tape the large envelopes, his big fingers kept getting in the way, making a mess. I walked over, "here, let me help you," I said.

"Alright here take this," he said, looking a little frustrated as he handed a big tape ball to me. I took the supplies to the counter and started taping the two envelopes, sealing them closed.

"Really, what are these?" I asked, real nice trying to use my information getting techniques. It had always been easy for me when trying to gather information for the government, but maybe those men were just smart geeks looking for attention. They had told me that I didn't have to sleep with the men to get what was needed. Now as I think about it they were always saying one thing and meaning anther. The government couldn't say sleep with them so they just brought you in hoping you would understand that you did what you had too to gain information. Quinn started talking, see you just have to ask and most men open up to you.

"I took these shots loaded with what they were pumping into us from the swamp where we were being held. I am sending them to a friend in Miami that works for a crime lab so he can run a few tests. We need to see what kind of combo, of drugs is in them. I took five shots; I am sending him two and two to my place in Miami, just in case. We need some kind of insurance. We will keep one with us, it seems to help us heal really fast," he said, moving to the door, "I'm going to put this in the mail right now, I'll be right back."

"Okay, I'll be on the top floor, see you up there," I said as I moved to the kitchen, to gather the food. It was weird that we both hadn't eaten that much in the past forty-eight hours and we were still going. These were some drugs, why hadn't we died like the rest of them? We had to find out what all this was about.

When Quinn returned I was in the summit room with the food spread out. I had bought a bottle of white wine to go with the fish. I made angel hair pasta with scallops and spinach in a light sauce. We ate in silence as we fell on the food. I didn't realize how hungry I was until we started and then I couldn't stop. It all tasted so good. I lay back in the soft chair sipping my wine.

"I am so full I can't move." The sun had set and darkness filled the room, making shadows from the candlelight lick the walls, filling the space with a almost romantic feel, that I quickly put to the back of my mind.

"That was really good, you're quite a cook Julie, and I wouldn't have thought you the type." He smiled between bites of his third helping.

"I'm sure I have many things that I am good at that would surprise most people." I set my wine down and rolled off the seat to the floor. I put my head on the floor and did a hand stand with ease. "Here is the topper." In a handstand I started doing push-ups. He clapped his hands, amused at my strength.

"That's really good. I have never seen a women do that before. Watch this!" He did the same thing and then lifted one hand and did push-ups in that poison with one hand.

"Show off. That is pretty incredible you're really strong, for a man that has that kind of natural body type."

"I think these shots have made me stronger. I feel like we were able to go longer with out food and I swear I can see better than before. We have healed faster than anything I have ever seen. These shots have made my senses better. What do you think? How is your hearing? Can you see farther? Are your reflexes quicker? Do your senses seem to be affected like mine?" Quinn asked, as he anther took a bite of food.

"I think you're right, but what about touch?" I said laughing as I ran my hand down his hard shoulder. His reaction was quick as he ran his hand down my leg and I felt my insides melt to his touch. I leaned my body into his and felt a surge of heat, bounce back and forth between the two of us. He moved away first as if he had been burned, leaving me missing his warmth.

"I guess all of the above." I said, moving back to the chair, gathering the dishes, preparing to leave the room, to calm my heart beat down. What was all that about? Had these shots increased my sex drive too?

"We need…to get cleaned up and get some rest. Did you want to use the bathroom first?" He asked. I just nodded and went down the stairs, acting like I wasn't just rejected again. How many times can this happen in one day. His small touch had unnerved me, I wondered if the drugs were making me feel hot too, I felt like I was having a hot flash and at my age I knew that it wasn't possible. It was a good explanation to avoid my reaction to him. If this was the case he must be feeling it too. Then I wondered if this was the effect of the shots then would I feel he same about him after they wore off. I thought about this as the water ran off my body, finally turning cold, making me realize that it was time to get out. After my shower, I felt clean and refreshed as I combed my hair. Quinn came in and started removing his clothes, it was time for me to leave the room, and just being this close to his nude body sent a tingle down my spine. When he was in the shower I snuck in and took all his clothes, tossing them in the washer with mine. Quickly before he got out of the shower, I jumped in bed before he came in the room. The light was muted but it was easy to see the well-shaped form of the Viking. His body was incredible, hard as stone, with every part in perfect proportion. The light gleamed off each curve causing ripples of muscle as he walked through the room. If it had been the old days I could see him dragging me off by my hair. What a sight he was, I could tell he knew I was watching him. He moved slowly like a large cat to the bed, pulling just the blanket up over him as he lay beside me. A fresh white sheet was all that separated our bodies as he pulled me in tight, against his hard bulk. My heart was beating too fast; I felt I was having a hot flash. I willed myself to calm down, trying not to show that I was reacting to his sexuality, which he had combed across the room. I tilted my head up and there he was right in my face, looking at me with those intense golden eyes.

"Don't think about it, you need rest," he said, as he ran his finger over my lip and moved in for the kill. His lips were soft but his kiss was firm as he pressed it on my willing lips. Then it was over and he closed his eyes, we just lay there. I don't know how I fell asleep, but the next morning when I awoke I was alone in bed. For a moment I thought I had dreamed it all and then remembered that we were still in danger, even hidden in our little paradise. Happy and rested from the past few days, I found Quinn downstairs dressed and drinking coffee.

"Your clothes are in the dryer," he said grinning.

"Thanks" I said, catching my reflection in the window, no wonder he was laughing at me. My hair was a mess, not being dried the night before and I trailed a long sheet in my wake as I moved. There was nothing like appearing cool in the morning in front of a hot man. After I dressed, with coffee in hand, I went into the room.

"I was thinking I will go and grab a paper, is there anything you need while I'm out?" I said, as I ran a hand through my unstable hair.

"No I'm good, I ate the left over pasta," Quinn said as he got up. He moved in front of me and took his small backpack, putting it on my back and adjusting it so the straps fit me.

"The money is in here," he showed me, "I know you women, you will need some thing to carry all your purchases in."

"Very funny," I said, "I'm not like most women."

"Well I know that," he smiled, "now get going and be really careful."

"I will, I won't be long," I said, as I put my hand on his large shoulder, raising on my tippy toes and kissed his check. I grabbed the keys, leaving before I could see his reaction. What was going on with me, he had already said he wasn't interested. I couldn't help it, he was a gentle giant and I wanted to help him stop hurting over what had happened in Brazil. Then I thought to myself, maybe I just had my own interest at heart. Thought again, no it was my weakness to be always drawn to people that I thought needed help, maybe that was part of the attraction.

In town, all was quiet; I picked up a paper from outside the small drug store and looked up as I saw some military trucks pass by. I wondered what was going on out here in the middle of nowhere; I didn't think there were any bases close by.

When returning to the beach house, I pulled on the street and saw two military trucks parked in front of the lighthouse. Oh Shit! They were looking for us! Turning on a side lane I got off the sandy road and pulled into a vacant house, parking the car. I got out and backtracked on foot, down to the street running across the dunes ducking in and out of houses staying out of sight, trying to get as close as possible. When I was across from the house, I watched and waited to see what was happening. I didn't have to wait long; Quinn was carried out fighting as he was pushed inside the back of truck. He was bound with shackles, it still took four men to move him and he wasn't going effortless. Large guns were aimed at him and the surrounding area, searching. Blood dripped from his forehead his clothes once clean were dusty and torn. I lay in the sand wondering how this special place could have turned so bad in just moments. I had been lucky that I had gone to the store or they would have had me in the back of the truck with Quinn. The motor vehicle pulled away, the other one moved down the street waiting, waiting for me. I ran backtracking across the dunes to the car, out of breath after running in the sand, sucking air as I jumped in and took off after the truck with Quinn. I was trying not to panic, but my heart was racing I couldn't lose him; I couldn't let them lock him back up. Who knows how many drugs it would take to finally kill him. I thought I had lost the truck as I turned a curve searching both ways, but there it was, keeping my distance I followed. They moved north down the road and pulled into an entrance of a state park, Fort Clinch. I watched them as they went through the checkpoint and waited until they were out of sight. I moved up to the booth to speak to the Ranger.

"Hello sir, I was wondering if you had any camp spaces available?"

"Yes, we are off season." A short man in his ranger outfit looked at the empty car and back at me.

"How much is it?" I asked, smiling up at the man dressed in the light brown and green uniform covered in patches.

"Are you tent camping or are you going to bring in a trailer?"

"I am going to tent camp, are there places in the woods?" I asked.

"Yes, it is $18 a night," he said.

"Okay," I handed him the money out of Quinn's stash. "I saw the military trucks, I read that you have tours of the old fort, is that part of a show?"

"Yes we usually do have tours, but right now the military is using the base for some kind of training so it is closed to the public. But we do have an alligator hike, you can spot them, some of the time. People also have had luck fishing from the pier, it goes way out from the beach," he said, trying to sell me on the idea of staying.

"Yes I remember I was here with my parents growing up. I'll take two nights." I smiled, transaction done, I moved inside the park. So they were using the base, someone had some big pull in the military to be able to occupy the old base. The fort had held many different military troops since the early 1700's. It is a brick fortress to the north of Fernandina beach. The old fort was on the northern point of Amelia Island, where it looks out over the sound. If I remembered right, it had in the past had seven or eight different flags fly over it. Later it was made into a state park and registered as a historical sight. As a child I remember the big canons still in their holds prepared for use facing the ocean ready for attack, they ran along all the walls facing the water. To get to the entrance you had to take a small road that went through the woods and over the dunes. You dropped down into a flat area where the structure rose out of the sand by the coast. Large cream-colored brick walls stood about twenty feet high with slots left open for guns to shoot through. It was impressive for something that had been built that many years ago.

I drove past the camping area father into the woods. Fort Clinch was about two to three miles from the entrance of the park. The trees were overgrown and formed a canapé over the road, blocking a lot of the light. As the sunrays streamed through I felt like I was in a far away place, in the middle of nowhere. I approached the turn off to the fort and keep driving past parking the car in a wooded area, off the shoulder of the road, out of sight.

Small trails went though the woods used for hikers and mountain bikes. I found one and followed it in the direction of the fort. The sun was getting high in the sky and I could feel the sweat as it drooped down my back under my clothes. I felt good and strong, I was in good shape. I left the path and made my way, crossing small trails left from the little creatures that inhabited the dunes. Up I climbed, I knew it was against the rules to be on them, they were used to block the island from erosion. Up high on top I could see down into the fort. The truck that had carried Quinn was parked under some trees, along with two others. So I was looking at four military trucks, counting the one parked at the beach house. That could mean eight to sixteen men inside, if not more. Everything within looked calm and from my position I couldn't see Quinn, but there was some activity, by one of the buildings. A few men could be seen lingering around the small enclosure that was shaded from the sun close to the back wall. How was I going to get inside and get Quinn out of there? It wouldn't be during the day, I would have to prepare for nighttime. A plan was forming in my mind but I had a lot to do before it got dark. I back tracked to the car and pulled down the road to the camping area.

******

Back at the base Commander Knocks sat at his desk, it was good to be back at the base, on the gulf side of Florida. Washington had always seamed to politically fast paced and he wanted nothing to do with anything that went on in the city or the people in it. He had been gone a few days and had hardly been missed. The only thing showing his absence was the pile of mail and paper work waiting for him. After all the years with the air force he had been given a desk job with little responsibility. He gave the impression of being in charge of an area that monitored big classified machines, making sure their temperature didn't get too high causing a burn out. The men that worked in that section did every thing like clockwork and left little for him to do. After catching up on all the forms that needed to be processed, it was time to go home. He decided to stay and work on his little project. He pulled out the list of names he wanted to run through the national computer. There was about twelve that he wanted to check on, all had gone to the Oasis club that night. He had a hunch that the one he was looking for had a fake name. He paced waiting while the computer did its job and ran them through the system. Ten minutes later he had his results. They were all clean except two men, one of them was Frank; the other was a tan man with nice highlighted thick hair. Let's see what we can do to find out if this is really you Frank, he said, to himself as he pulled out a paper bag that contained the sealed glass, the one he had taken from Frank at the club.

He got up and went to the base's lab; it had emptied out for the night. He looked down the hall, no one was around, and the Commander ran his ID card through the computer lock and the green light buzzed. Inside the room was dark, he moved over to the cases searching for the finger print kits, cursing when he bumped into a table and had to wait to see if he was discovered. He found a small desk light, turned it on and worked quickly; he wasn't expecting anyone to be coming down his end of the hall, at this time of night, but who knows. He brushed the dust over the prints on the glass and was happy when something appeared. Covering the print with clear tape he removed it from the glass and carefully smoothed it over a white piece of paper. The Commander smiled to himself, it was fun playing Jr. detective after hours, anything different from the busy work that he was surrounded with everyday. He closed down the room leaving it as he had found it and moved down the hall to where the duty officer was working at the desk. He had seen her around but didn't even know her name.

"Hi, I was wondering if you could run this print through the computer and see if there's a match." The moment he had rounded the corner she had been on her feet. Seeing his uniform she knew at once his rank.

"Yes sir Commander. I'll do it right now if you want to wait," she said.

"If it is not...any trouble..., I can wait." She took the paper and moved to a machine that took a picture of the print and put it into the network. It didn't take long to get a hit, up popped a drivers license of my friend Frank. Frank Burns was a retired politician for the state of Georgia. It looked like now he was a registered lobbyist working with scientists on patents when they came up with for new drugs. He lived in Washington DC in a nice area of the city where he ran his office, out of his home.

Commander Knocks thanked the duty officer and went back to his office. He got rid of the list of all the people that checked out. He copied the photo of the tan man with his fake name and ID. He wondered who this nameless man was he looked powerful. The Commander put the information he had found, along with the man's face to memory, tomorrow was another day. Then he copied all the information on Frank Burns along with his photo and put everything in his floor safe. Now he felt a sense of relief, just by knowing who one of the players was made him feel better. He went home to watch TV and have a beer.

CHAPTER FIVE

A sinister light faded through the trees at the camp sight. It had been a full day of getting prepared, to break out Quinn. I settled down to rest, waiting for the right time, to make my move. The best time would be at 4am, most of the soldiers would be asleep and the entrance to the park would be open soon. The gates were locked at 8pm at night until the park opened in the morning. I tried to make myself rest, but it was hard to turn off my brain. What was I doing? This was a foolish plan, who did I think I was? Why didn't I call for help? But whom would I call? Who could be trusted? Quinn was the only one at this point that fell into that category and he was being held prisoner by the government. If you can't trust the government that trained you, whom could you trust? How could this have happened? I heard a sound outside and my blood pressure rose as I sat up straight without making any noise, someone was at my camp sight. I listened, my ears straining. A growl, thank you I hadn't been found. I slowly unzipped the flap of the tent; sitting on the picnic bench sat two very large raccoons. They were as big as dogs and looked hungry. Heart racing I zipped up the flap, laying down and waited. Soon they moved on and I heard them a few camp sights down the path. I hated raccoons they were always getting into things and tearing trash up. In Kansas when I was young, my parents put food in the garage for the dogs. Sometimes coming home late I would come face to face with a raccoon or possum eating the dog food and have to tip toe by as they watched with their beady little eyes.

At 3:30 am I made my move, I was dressed, the car was loaded and ready, I started the engine and moved down the road, towards the fort. The street was very dark and full of shadows there were no lights except for the headlights of the VW Bug I drove. I tried not to let my mind, take a trip and freak me out. For a moment I was scared out of my wits and had to control my mind, you're a Marine act like it. A sign said the fort was up ahead; I turned off the car lights. I traveled forward slowly as my eyes adjusted to the darkness. Passing the entrance, I moved to a small drive of the abandoned ranger station and parked the car. Gathering my gear, I stepped to the trail, covering the distance fast as I found the sand dunes ahead. Working my legs hard I climbed to the top of a sandy dune and took out my binoculars, looking down into the camp. Light shined from two areas, one looked like an old bunkhouse for soldiers, the other an aged building that looked like it had been used for making bullets and horseshoes? I could see old machinery along with two guards posted. Bingo that had to be were Quinn was, okay time to go.

I moved through the dunes and trees surrounding the fort. I knew there was no way I could go in the front door so I had brought some climbing gear. I moved down the wall at the corner closest to the beach, away from the area I believed the soldiers were at. I had a heavy hook, like what you used as an anchor on a boat with a rope tied to it. Swinging it over my head, I let it go over the side of the wall. It came falling back down, shit, the wall had to be twenty feet high. I stepped back and twirled it over my head like a cowboy roping a calf, aimed and let it go. This time it went over the wall, I heard a clang and held my breath. I waited and didn't hear any movement inside, and started pulling on the rope slowly. It moved, and arm-by-arm, I reeled it in, finally, it took hold. Yes, okay now, I had to go up the wall. In training I had learned to climb a rope, with the flat wall it wasn't hard to get to the top. I saw when I pulled myself over the side, that I was barely hooked to an old brick, if I had weighed more, the anchor wouldn't have held. Pleased with myself, I attached my rope to a nearby cannon and tossed the end over the side out of sight. I moved across the top of the wall, it was about ten feet wide made out of light bricks that had been bleached by the sun over the past 100 years. I followed the ramp made of old bricks that lead down to the floor of the fort. Small buildings arose on each side giving the appearance of a small town, from long ago. I moved to a building that had some dim light glowing from the windows. Looking closer, it was the officers housing used in the 1800's now shown to the tourists so they could see how it was back then. Through the window, eight men lay in the tiny bunk beds build of wood, their feet hanging over the edges of the straw mattresses. It wasn't comfortable back in those days; a few of the men had taken the floor. All was quiet.

I took some bungee cords out of my bag and rigged the doors closed. It wouldn't hold too long but just in case, it would slow them down. I moved to the side of the armory and tried to think how to play this, there were two guards sitting on the ground, leaning against the building. One I could take but two was going to be a problem if it was going to be fight. I put my bag down, put a knife inside my black running tights, fluffed my hair and moved to the front of the building.

"Hello guys." They both jumped to their feet, guns in hand. "Put the guns down guys, I didn't mean to scare you," I said, they looked unsure, but I could tell they thought me harmless with my tights and running bra and round curvy ass. I smiled at the two soldiers; thinking please, let this work.

“Where did you come from? What are you doing here?” The bigger of the two men stood taking charge and checked me out. I watched as he gave me the up and down stopping on my butt.

“What did you think, I jumped the wall? I was hired by one of your officers to help you guys release some tension.” The bigger man smiled.

“You don’t look like the type to be paid for,” he said, as I faked insult, I did a grinding motion with my hips as I bent over in a slow movement.

“Time’s money boys, who is first?” I said, looking into the eyes of the large one, knowing he was the leader of the two men. He took the challenge and wanted to play along.

“Okay I’ll go first, Pete you stand guard and I’ll be back,” he said, “Watch him,” He said, motioning to Quinn. I then allowed my eyes to look to the area he was being held. He didn’t look good and rage could be seen bubbling under the surface as he watched me.

“Come on soldier around here so we can have some privacy.” He followed me around to the back of the structure and I let him press up against me as he rubbed my hips and breasts with his clumsy hands. I kissed his neck and whispered, let me; I pulled his paints down to his ankles. Moving behind him, I ran my hand over his abs, pushing him to his knees. Before he knew what was happening, I had him pinned to the ground hog tied with a pair of my underwear taped in his mouth. I pulled him to his feet, dragged up his pants and tied him to a tree. His eyes looked wild with disbelief, I smiled and told him to “relax, if I wanted to kill you I would have.” Back in front of the structure, I found the other guard leaning against the wall; he didn’t look pleased when he saw I was alone. “He had to go to the bathroom,” I said, “I’ll give you yours here if you don’t mind your friend watching,” I said, motioning to Quinn as his eyebrow rose. The soldier looked like he didn't know what to do, so I moved to where he was standing and stoked his gun.

"Don't worry, I will be gentle," I said.

I took his hand and put it on my breast.

"It's not that, I shouldn't...leave my post," he stammered.

"We won't." I took the gun out of his hand and laid it down on a workbench.

"Here, so you're not nervous in front of the prisoner." I walked over and acted like I was covering Quinn's face with a towel as I slipped my knife into his hand. Turning to the young man, I danced over moving my hips, he was laughing feeling the moment. Acting like I was going to touch myself, I had all his attention. Quinn cut the ropes that were holding him and knocked the guard out, he fell hard to the ground. We both tied him quickly and I pulled out one more pair of panties and put them in his mouth and taped it shut.

Quinn was trying not to laugh, "Is this what the government taught you? Well I'll just have to call you the underwear dancer," he laughed.

"Very funny, you better be kind to your rescuer. Now stop making jokes Mr. joke man and come on. This is the second time I have saved your ass or is it the third? But who's counting?"

He slapped me on the butt, "I like the tights."

"Quit fooling around, let's get out of here, and by the way they are running pants!" I said as I moved along the wall to the corner of the building, where I had left my rope. We slid down the wall and ran across the dunes and through the trees. The VW was still where I had left it, behind the dark undergrowth. With the lights off I drove toward the camp sight. As I turned toward the tented area, Quinn gave me a look.

"Don't you think we need to get some distance between us and them?" he asked, acting like I had no brains.

"No, I think we need to be playing offense now and find out what is happening. They will think that we left and will be looking for us. This way we can spy on them and find out what this is all about. I planted a few bugs inside of the fort, so all we have to do is listen when they wake up and find you gone."

"Well the mind of a women always surprises me, good job, I'm impressed," he said, I drove past the camp sight to a wooded area by the beach and hid the car. We walked back to the camp area; he looked at the sagging tent.

"I see you're better at making plans than putting up a tent. You have that top part backwards," he chuckled "this is the most fun I have had running from the bad guys in a long time."

"Alright, fix the top and get in the tent, the bugs are biting me,"' I said as I jumped into the small enclosure. He did what he was told and I could tell he was impressed by the whole set up. The air mattress was full, the bed made, and listening gear ready and on, the lights and small Coleman stove and a cooler stocked with food sat to the side of the bed.

"You have been busy," he said as he took some water and paper towels and cleaned the cuts that were new left from the struggle earlier, but already healing.

"Lets rest a few hours until they get up.

We will hear them, when they start moving around."

******

Washington DC —Two Days Ago

"Sir, Senator, a Frank Burns is here in the waiting room." The senator looked up from behind his large desk, what was he doing here he thought! He must have made a face, because the women at the door looked at him with question

"Do you want me to get rid of him sir?" The women asked, pausing in the doorway.

"No Marline, thank you, just send him in, it will be alright," he said, standing up, he moved to the sideboard pouring himself a shot of old scotch. Frank entered the room with heavy footsteps moving to the desk, panic in his stride.

"We have a problem," he said, the senator put his hand up for silence and moved to the door, making sure it was closed all the way.

"You need to keep your voice down! What do you think you are doing here! I told you never to come here and here you are busting in my office! Have you gone and lost your mind?" The senator's voice was curt and anger flowed out of his pores.

"Look, there wasn't time to go through the motions! This is urgent! All shit has broken loose!" Frank said as he moved and poured himself a shot of the scotch, swallowing it all in one gulp. He wiped the sweat off his forehead and stared at the senator with his beady little eyes, saying I'm going to beat the shit out of you.

"Alright calm the F…down! Tell me what has happened," said the Senator, trying to remain in control of the situation.

"Our little lab in Georgia has had a problem! Out of the twenty solders we took down there, 18 have died from the shots," he screamed.

"Now we knew that was a possibility when all this started.

Some more will die before the drug is refined. Now calm down." The senator said as he freshened his glass. "Put together some more files and meet with our commander again and get some new soldiers down there."

"You don't understand, other than the 18 that didn't make it; the two that did have escaped and for some reason we had a extra soldier that went with them." We don't even know where he came from." Frank said as he paced the room. "We are going to be ruined."

"What are you talking about, Escaped! You said you had the lab taken care of; all small details were under control. How could anyone get away? This is not going to come back on me, you need to get your ass down there and take care of this problem," the senator yelled.

"I have been working on it and have caught one of them. They somehow made it out of the swamps.

We are looking for the girl and the other man right now. They seam to have disappeared into thin air but I will find them," Frank said, walking over and pouring anther drink, downing it.

"We are using a girl and she is the one giving you grief. You better get down there today and put a sealed lid on this. Then send twenty more soldiers to Doctor Belvar at the lab. My sources tell me that, a new batch of drugs, have just arrived. If these two didn't die from the doses we need to know what was done differently, we need a sample of their blood. Find them! They are the answer to refining it. If we can get it to work, it is going to be worth lots of money.

I hope you are on a plane, within the next hour. Now just remember next time, to go through channels to reach me, don't ever come here again," the Senator said as he walked Frank to the door, that lead out of the office. Back at his desk he looked in a small phone book and put his finger on a name—Steve Smith, he had worked with him in the past. After things quiet down he was going to need his services again. He looked at the name and closed the book knowing that he would clean things up when it came time.

******

Frank made a few phone calls, one of them to Commander Knocks, he left a message to meet him next week in Washington. He was on the plane two hours later, going to visit an old fort.

CHAPTER SIX

I was awakened out of my slumber by voices, they sounded close, and I froze until I realized the noise was coming from the bugging equipment. I looked at my watch and it was 6:15 am. Banging and the sound of yelling along with breaking glass came through loud and clear. When I planted the bugs I must have put them in good locations, it was my tendency to over do, more was always better, than not enough. I had attached at least 15 different devices all over the fort to make sure I got the information I needed. Quinn was awake looking in the cooler for some food. The day before when I was waiting I had made a whole loaf of bread worth of sandwiches, with all kinds of lunchmeat. Along with my bottled Starbucks coffee and fruit salad, we would be set for a few days of waiting. I pulled out two pairs of headphones and plugged them in and handed one to Quinn. This way we could keep the noise down and still hear outside at the same time. At the moment it sounded like a lot of scrambling around. I guessed they were breaking out of my bungee cord hook-up. Soon after the guards were found and I could hear moaning as they were untied.

"What happened here?" An officer was yelling.

"It was a women," the guard said, embarrassment in his voice. "She said, she was a gift from you, for all of the long hours Pete and I have been watching the big man. After I was tied up, I knew it was a lie, she was so convincing and really strong," the solder said, shame in his voice.

"So what you are saying is, a women by herself was able to put both of you out of commission and escape with the prisoner. She was so quiet and stealth that she surprised you both and tied you up. What is that in your hand Pete?" The officer asked with a tone that you just wanted to obey.

"Panties sir," Pete said, looking down into his hand.

"Panties? Where did you get the panties Pete?" The officer asked.

"She put them in my mouth sir," he said, and I could feel his disgrace in his voice. I was feeling a little bad for the young men.

"You keep panties of the women that you have slept with, not the ones that kicked your ass. Both of you move out, get cleaned up and fall in at 1900 hours."

I looked over at Quinn; he was holding his gut laughing so hard. I put my hand over his mouth to stop the noise. He licked my hand, "Damn you're nasty," I said. "Get yourself together," I wiped my wet hand off on my jeans.

"Now you can't say that that wasn't funny!" He smiled, laughter in his voice.

"You're right, but keep it down laughing man, I can't hear!" Why was he acting so silly? Sometimes men think stupid things were soooo funny. I had just used what I had at the moment. I didn't like the laughing at my expense.

Inside the officer quarters I could hear the man in charge talking to someone else. "We need to wait, he will be here within the hour and then we will try to find them. They couldn't' have gotten far, there are only so many highways out of the area. North, south or west it won't be hard we will have the police looking for the car," he said.

"Who is the man that is coming?" The other man said

"He is some politician, I think he used to be Georgia's state representative. He is giving the orders for some reason, I don't know why because he never served in the military. It is all really weird. The guy we were holding was some special forces or agent; don't even know why we were holding him. Doesn't seem right, I'm glad he got away. But that's between us," the officer said.

"Hey my lips are sealed, I agree with you," the other man said.

"When the politician gets here lets try to find out what they were holding him for. I just want to know, he was one of us," the officer said.

"But on a lighter note, who was the woman that got him out of here?"

"Maybe his girlfriend," the other said.

"Maybe she's a agent too?" the officer said.

"I don't think so. Who would carry extra panties to stuff in men's mouths." The other man laughed, "Did you see how horrified those two were. You know I wanted to bust out laughing, but I knew you had to do your job."

"It's okay, I wanted to brake out laughing myself. Ha ah ha I wish I could have saw her, they said she was really hot," the officer said.

"Today looks like it won't be boring," the other man said with amusement in his voice. "It might be fun to find her so we can get a look at her."

I popped Quinn's earpiece out of his ear, "I guess I was a hit. While we are waiting for the politician to get here, why don't you tell me about yourself?"

"What do you want to know? He asked as he downed a turkey sandwich.

"What do you want to tell me? How long have you been working for the government? Does this crazy stuff happen to you all the time? You seem to enjoy it a little too much."

"Sorry classified" he smirked.

"Alright tell me something that is not classified!" He was starting to get on my nerves.

"Okay, I was in the Air Force, my job was to go behind enemy lines when one of our planes went down. My team would rescue and take the technology secrets off the American aircrafts before the enemy could get to the plane.

"Did you ever get hurt?" I asked

"Some times we would be under all kinds of incoming fire. One time as we were trying to get out, I got hit in the ankle. It wasn't a fun day, hiking over the hills with my shirt around my ankle and hobbling my way out," he said, as he lifted his pants leg, pulled down his sock, and showed me the big scar.

"That must have bled a lot," I said, looking at the scar tissue.

"Yah, you know flesh wounds, they bleed more than they do damage, like if you get a cut on your ear it will bleed forever. But it did hurt a lot the next day. What about you? Any scars?"

"Mine aren't on the outside," I said, looking away not wanting to talk about myself.

"Come on, talk, I have told you something that not many know about me unless they were with me at the time. What about you? What can you tell that's not classified?"

"Mine run deep and I already told you about my brother."

"Well when you're ready, you can tell me," he said patting my hand.

"Cut that out! Don't try and be nice to me now! Alright! My parents were killed back when I was in high school." He stopped all laughter gone from his face watching me.

"What happened? Was it an accident? He asked, concern now in his voice as he waited.

"I was told it was some random break in, someone searching for money or things, to sell for drugs. At the time, I believed the police. What else could it have been? I was at school that day and came home to find the street full of police cars. They wouldn't let us near the house, so I sat on the sidewalk for hours watching, I think I was in shock. I wanted to go in and see myself; it didn't seem real until I could see what had happened. Afterwards, I put everything that was left from the house in a storage locker; my brother and I were sent to live with an aunt. When I turned 21, I was given a key to a locked trunk that had been my parents; it is still sitting in the smoky smelling storage unit.

Inside I found papers and passports, my parents were or at least used to be, Russian citizens. I put them back where I found them and closed the storage unit and haven't returned. I had always thought my parents were Americans like everyone else. But the more I thought about it we never had relatives that we would spend time with us, like other families.

As a child you think all families are like yours. Thinking about it now, the aunt we went to live with was not really my aunt; she didn't look anything like my family. We were all blond, blue and brown eyed and she had very dark brown hair, dark eyes, almost black. I always just thought that my parents were scientists that worked for NASA. I put the trunk back in the storage unit in Andover Kansas and haven't touched it since. I never told my brother what I thought I had found. I think that my parents were Russian sleepers in the United States or they were stealing technology and forwarding it on, to Russia. It sounds far fetched now thinking about it, but at the time I wanted it to be more than it was to explain the reason they had died. I don't know, maybe some day I will look more closely at the contents of the trunk, but in the meantime, the past is locked up. Now you know my biggest secret, you're the only one I have told, I have never talked about this to anyone," I rested my head on my arm not wanting to look up, I wasn't sure if he was going to judge me for what I thought my parents had done. Instead he grabbed me up in his big strong-arms and held me tight, patting my head.

"I don't need any pity," I said trying to get away. He just held on to me tighter, I gave up and just let him. Maybe it was healthy, to finally tell someone.

"No pity, I just thought you could use a hug," Quinn said, as he tried to look underneath, my hair, to see my eyes. He pulled my head up, so I would look at him.

"Thank you," I said, he released his hold and I rolled off the air mattress to the hard floor, of the tent. "Here," I handed him his earpiece and put mine in my ear. I thought to myself, Okay that was enough talk to last a while. Why did I tell Quinn anything? I had decided that I would never tell anyone about my parents and here I was blabbing. Someday I would have to face what was in that trunk, but not today. I pushed it to the back of my mind and concentrated on what I was hearing.

Our politician had arrived and he sounded like he was blowing a gasket. He was yelling at anyone who would listen.

"How did he get away? How does a girl the size of a thirteen-year-old come in here, take out two of your men, lock the rest up and take off with your prisoner into the sunset? What are you doing to find them!

They have to be found!" Frank said heavy footsteps could be heard as he paced the room. The officer's tone said he thought Frank needed to calm down; the tone that officers have, that you just do what they say with no questions asked.

"We will find them, we have already called in local law enforcement. They are watching all the highways out of town. They only got a two and a half hour head start. So it is not hard to predict how far they can get in that amount of time sir. We will find them."

Frank seemed to calm down.

"Okay officer, good job."

"Sir if you don't mind my asking, what is this all about?" He asked, Frank paused thinking how much he could tell without saying too much.

"Well, we have been trying to find a cure for some kind of virus he picked up in Brazil and we are producing a drug that will help him. He is just not so sure that he wants to be helped. He still works for the government and his blood has the key to the cure, for the virus.

When we find him we might just have to send him down to Rio De Janeiro to our lab down there." That was as close to the truth as Frank was going to say, he couldn't say that they were trying to build a military weapons with the solders becoming the weapons themselves.

"Okay sir, I will leave you to rest after your trip. I will let you know when we find them." The solder said "good day sir" and left the room.

Quinn and I looked at each other. "What does Brazil have to do with this drug they have used on us? They are making it down there?" I asked, Quinn was quite thinking, and then I could see the light bulb go off over his head.

"I think that information might tie into the case that I had been working on down in Rio. Remember I told you I had been watching ships go to Brazil from the Miami shipyard. On the return we thought it was drugs and money coming back in to the United States, though Miami, but we never found anything. I wonder if the drugs we were following are the same ones that are being manufactured in Rio. We have to find out, gather your things." He started picking up what we needed to bring from the tent.

"Where are we going?" I asked.

"To Jacksonville to catch a boat to Miami," he said.

I stuffed everything into Quinn's backpack and started to walk towards the car.

"The car is no use anymore, come on," he said. We headed to the beach and were soon running south on the wet sand by the surf. We closed in on the area where the beach houses were and crept up the sand in-between the dwellings. Our lighthouse could be seen down the shore, white against the blue sky. We made sure if they were watching for us they wouldn't see us. We cut around the corner and found what Quinn had been looking for. In a carport of a vacant house was a large Harley motorcycle. I thought the chain holding it to the side of the house would stop us. But not Quinn, he found some tools and quickly got the chain loose. He opened the small hood and moved some wires around, he looked like he knew what he was doing. I had only saw this done on TV and was surprised when it started up. Engine running, Quinn grabbed the helmets off the sidewall, by the door. He slammed one down on my head and I felt my brains jiggle in my skull.

"Whoops sorry, I'm a little strong these days," he said, at the look on my face, I hit him in the arm.

"Jump on." On the back of the bike I held on tight to the Viking. The air whipped my fine hair around on my face feeling like bugs.

All I could do was close my eyes and listen to the wind as it hit my helmet. The soft scent of salt water faded into the distance as we found the road to Jacksonville.

******

BASE IN FLORIDA

It was months end and the Commander was early for work, he had make an effort to get the work ready to turn in. The yellow light was flashing on his phone, and told him he had a message. Pressing the button he heard a voice that he didn't think he would ever here again. "Commander, this is Frank, I need to meet with you again in Washington, come to the same place, same time, this coming Saturday night. If you can't make it please contact me. If you can make it, I will see you Saturday." He looked at his calendar, he had three days until Saturday; he sat back down at his desk thinking, this time he would have a plan. Opening up his floor safe he pulled out the picture of Frank, the tan man and the fake drivers license. Who are you? This time he would find out. Finishing his paper work, putting it in the out box, he went to take a walk. A plan was forming; he would have to wait until after hours to gather what was needed. His feet went to the beat of his heart as his excitement grew. He went back to his office to write up the orders, making a few phone calls and reserve the airline tickets.

The day passed quickly and the offices at his end of the building had cleared out. He went to the lab and got a fingerprint kit, it was small and wouldn't take up much room. He got a mini recorder with some tapes and moved toward his office. As he passed the area where the fingerprints are taken, the same duty officer was working the desk. She smiled at him and stood a little taller as he approached. He walked up to the desk; an idea had come to him when he saw the women officer.

His strategy might work, but what would she think, she was an attractive women.

"Hello," he said.

"Hello Commander Knocks, what can I do for you this evening?" She asked.

"I'm sorry, I don't know your name young lady." He smiled.

"It's Sheri Long, sir," she said.

"Sheri this is going to sound really weird but I need someone that looks like you and is about your age to do some undercover work for me this Saturday in Washington DC. Now I know what you are thinking, this old guy is hitting on me, I would love to hit on you sometime, but this isn't the time. I am working on a case and it would take someone that looks like you to get the information."

"Sir, I'm not sure I am allowed to have the time off to do this kind of work," Sheri said looking a little nervous. "This is highly irregular, sir."

"I can put in for the orders and it would be okay. What I need to know is if you are willing to do this kind of work. You would be paid for your time two upgrades higher. What do you think?" He said hopefully, He could see her really considering the idea. He didn't want her to imagine he was making a play for her. Now that he looked at her she really was good looking. She had long brown hair, at this moment it was pulled into a bun, a real pretty face, about 5'7'-5'9', and very long legs. She looked like she was slender with an athletic build. Yes, she would work out nicely, perfect bait for lusty men.

"Okay if it is real orders I can do this, the Air Force will have to pay all the expenses up front on their end and three level upgrades," she said, looking pleased with herself for having thought of it off the top of her head.

"That won't be a problem, we will leave Friday morning and return Sunday afternoon. I will get the orders in place and assign someone to replace you here at the desk," he said.

"What will I be doing?" She asked.

"You will help me get a man's fingerprints so we can find out who he is." Suddenly she understood and relaxed. Sheri remembered looking up the prints in the computer for him. He did need her help, this was an adventure, cool. She looked up as he watched her process the information.

"You're going to need to get something to wear that looks like a strip club...worker or street walker, um...like you have sex on your mind." He was having trouble getting it out. She smiled at him and patted his hand. He pulled out three hundred dollars and put it in her palm. "For the outfit."

"I understand, don't worry I won't let you down I will look the part." She saw relief crosses his face; he didn't have to say anymore. People of her parents' generation was a little uptight, when it came to talking about sex.

"Write down your phone number and I will call to let you know what time I will send a driver to pick you up Friday." He left, feeling good, it would be better to have a partner, that they didn't know about, just like Frank had the tan man.

CHAPTER SEVEN

We had pulled into an underground parking structure in the basement of a high-rise building, off of Biscayne Blvd. Quinn and I went up the elevator to the eighth floor, at the end was a wooden door that opened up into a well furnished, bachelor pad, and windows ran along the entire wall of the living room. Glass doors exposed a patio with chest high railings that overlooked the bay. I sat down on the comfortable outdoor furniture that filled the long balcony that ran the length, of the condo. It was beautiful, large ships, freighters, motorboats of every kind could be seen from this view bouncing on the waves as they made their way in the shipping lanes to their docks.

"It is so beautiful. Is this where you live?" I asked, I could tell he was happy with my reaction to his good taste.

"It is one of my hideouts, I'm glad you like it." He smiled "We will be safe here, no one knows it is mine; I have a different name on it. The bathroom is over there," he said pointing, "why don't you clean up, I need to take care of a few things," he said as he moved to the phone.

"Okay, sounds good," I said as I went in the direction of the bathroom. I was starting to wonder who this Quinn was, how could he afford a place like this? It had to be a cool million. All thoughts left me as I soaked in the hot water of the large white tub. I felt calm and relaxed when I finished. I found a large fluffy white robe waiting for me on the back of the door and I wrapped it around me and took all my clothes to the washer. I felt so much better, now I just needed some food. I found

Quinn in the kitchen cooking eggs, bacon and toast, when I smelled the coffee I thought, heaven.

"I made a few calls when you where in the bath, remember those shots that I sent to my friend at the crime lab. Well he found out what was in the syringes'." He paused; I could tell that he was trying to break it to me softly.

"Just say it, what was in them!" I knew whatever he said; I was going to be mad. I didn't like drugs.

"What he did was put the sample through a machine called a mass spectrometer. It breaks down the chemical makeup of the substance giving a identifying fingerprint of what is in the sample."

"Okay got it, he found what we were given. What was it?" I was feeling impatient and wanted him to get to the point.

"It was a combo of chemicals that cause addiction and strength that work with continued high levels of endorphins released into the body," he said.

"What are you saying? It sounds like some kind of crack to me," I said starting to freak out. I didn't like anything to control me. Even in high school I wouldn't try things like everyone else because I heard that some were highly addictive.

"That's what my friend said, he thought it was combined with the elements of a street drug, in liquid form along with extras that he hadn't totally identified. The combination might be what causes the results we received. He said it was some unknown kind of chemical, that he had no idea of what it was, something new. He thought the others soldiers had died because it was an overdose. He told me you were okay because you weren't given as much because of your lower weight and being a girl. I was all right because I am so much bigger than the men they had locked up. I guess it would take much more of the drug to off me, I am about 60 pounds heavier than the men that were brought in. It has been almost a week, how do you feel? I still feel as strong as I was before; I wonder how long it takes to wear off or if it does?" Quinn looked thoughtful. "He said he thought it worked with our DNA making changes, so we really are the experiment to see if are enhancements stay with us, I think they might.

"Great, now I am a strong crack head!" I said, feeling angry for what had been done to me, by our government. I wondered how high up this went and, I was going to find out. "Yah, it is staying the same with me, not getting stronger but not getting weaker either. What are we going to do now?" I asked.

"I have been thinking I need to go down to the port of Miami and check on a ship to see if it is still moving back and forth to South America. If it is, I am going to go back down to Rio; I need to see where they are manufacturing these drugs. We need to know if they are the same ones that were used on us," he said, not looking at me. Something was up I could feel it.

"The Biscayne Bay is known for drugs coming into the United States. It is so busy that boats can slip in and out undetected, they move up the Miami River where there are thousands of private docks where they can get lost. Gangs, who know what is in the shipments, rob the boats. Nothing has been reported to the law enforcement. There are areas around the port of Miami that are full of all kinds of gangs made up of immigrants from Latin America, the Caribbean and Honduras. It is dangerous and if this is the case, I don't want to put you in danger. These drugs can't get into the main stream population." Quinn moved around making himself busy cleaning up the kitchen.

"What are you saying? YOU'RE going down to Brazil! Don't you mean WE are going to Rio?" Now I was getting mad, I looked down at my hand and it was shaking, going to the place where I always carried my gun. He wasn't going to leave me here, either he took me or I would go alone. I've just about had it with men trying to protect me. I could take care of myself. I wasn't having it! Don't make me mad; you won't like it, I thought, I might look calm on the outside, but inside a rage was building and he didn't want to cross me.

"Look Julie, it is safe here at my condo, you could wait for me here, I would be in contact." I could tell he was getting upset; the temperature was rising inside the condo. "I just don't want anything to happen to you, people are dead already." He moved to stand in front of me trying to plead his case.

"Now look here, this involves me just as much as it does you and you're not going without me. Who do you think got you out of a tight fit, how many times? I won't slow you down; just remember I am a Marine. I know you like me and want me to be safe, that is sweet but I am going!" I yelled.

"I didn't say I liked you," he said under his breath. I put my hand on his arm and he stood motionless. I knew he had to be thinking of the girl he had dated and died. That had nothing to do with me; I had to see this through for many reasons.

"It's going to be ok," I whispered. He just nodded and I hugged him around the waist and he petted my hair. He pulled away quickly from my embrace almost shoving me to the ground as I regained my balance.

"I have to go down to a private dock just up the Miami River from the bay. It is not far I'll be back in a few hours. There is a pool on the roof that is pretty nice if you want to use it while I'm gone. It has an infinity pool, you know the kind where the water comes to the edge, and it over looks the bay. Sometimes photo shoots done up there, that is fun to watch." He said trying to sound like he wasn't bothered.

"Okay, I will see you in a couple hours." Then he was gone and I was alone. Twenty minutes later, I was in a taxi on the way to South Beach. It was a nice sunny day outside; I sat in back enjoying the ride. It was a weekday; there were not too many people, on the street. The taxi pulled up in front of the Chase Bank, I told the driver to wait, as I went inside, I walked up to the desk, thinking of what I would say.

"I need to get into a safety deposit box," I said, the clerk took out a file box.

"What is the name on the account?" She asked.

"Matt Turner" I said.

"Is your name on the account?" The clerk asked.

"Yes, it should be," I said, hopeful now. I didn't think of that. She found the card with Matt's name and looked at it.

"What is your name?" She asked.

"Julie Redford," I answered.

"Yes here you are you have some ID? Okay looks good, follow me." I was taken to an open vault; she had her key and turned it in a box. I handed her mine from around my neck and she turned it and opened the box. Inside was a metal container that she handed me and directed me to a small room with a curtain as the door, I went inside, pulled the curtain tight and just stood looking at the box. After a few seconds I opened it and out fell an envelope addressed to one and me addressed to his mother. There was about five thousand in cash, with my name written on it. I took everything jamming it into my large shoulder bag. The taxi was still out front waiting as I stepped onto the hot pavement. I directed the man to take me to a boutique two blocks from the beach to buy some clothes. I found a few bathing suits and a summer dress, along with shorts and a few tops. At the last moment I saw a beautiful white dress with material, which just flowed with movement. It was in my size and I thought what the hell and tossed it on the counter Along with a straw hat that I added to the stack. I was out the door in thirty minutes and headed back to the condo to prepare, for my journey to Brazil.

As I opened the door, movement could be perceived from inside. Someone was rushing toward the entrance; I dropped my bags ready to fight. Whoops, it was Quinn and he had a mean look on his face. I picked up the bags.

"Honey I'm home?"

He stood looking at me, "I was worried, and I don't like feeling that way!"

"I'm sorry, I had a few things to do before we left." I could tell he had calmed down and was just glad that I had returned okay.

"I had to visit Matt's bank in South Beach and look I have cash." It was hard to be happy when you thought about where it came from. I dumped the contents of my bag out and started going through all the papers. "This has to go out in the mail," I said and handed him the letter addressed to Matt's mom. He nodded and went to the hall and put it in the box. When he came back I had the envelope with my name on it, I ripped it open and looked inside. There was one-piece paper explaining why we had the same orders and the conversation between him and Commander Knocks who was at a base in Florida. Also a few pages of research on the man that he had done after meeting him, in Washington.

"He met with the man that gave the orders sending me to the lab in Georgia." I handed Quinn the information for him to take a look at. "Matt's job was to watch and protect me. Now he is dead and here I am alive." I was trying not to get upset, but it made me sick. "He says here that this Commander was having trouble following orders and had called him in to help."

The letter continued: Julie, if you are reading this letter something has happened to me. None of it is your fault; I came at my own free will. You know how it is when you sign on. Your life can be in danger at any time and you prepare your mind for it.

Be careful, your friend Matt.

I dropped the letter on the table and went into the bedroom. I had to be alone for a moment and lay on the large guest bed and hugged one of the soft pillows to my chest and cried for the lose of Matt. He had been a good friend and he wasn't going to die for nothing, I would make sure of that! I pulled myself together and went back into the living room. Quinn was cooking some stir-fry with chicken and vegetables. I was glad he had just let me get under control on my own, sometimes when people are nice when you are feeling bad, it just makes it worse. I picked up a scrape of paper off the floor and read:

Commander Knocks = Nick Sanson

A phone number said, if you need help call. The name of a club the date, time and table beside the name. I wondered what that met?

"Did you see this?" I said, holding up the paper written on hotel stationary."

"No what is it?" He asked as he flipped the food around the pan.

"I think we have a phone number of the man that sent out the orders. Should we call him or wait?" I asked.

"I think we should wait until we find out more information in Brazil. Today I found the dock that I had been watching, there were armed guards hanging around out of sight. The boat was gone but I found this, he handed me part of a box. The cardboard, had a business logo on it, the writing was in Portuguese. Lets see if we can find out if this company is the same one our drug came from. Then we will have more information when we talk to him, we will know how involved he really is."

"You're right, that's a good plan. So we are leaving tomorrow night on the red eye? How long of a flight is it? I asked.

"It's nine hours from Miami, we have to switch planes in San Polo, Brazil. Be sure you leave anything that you can't afford to lose here, just in case. No real jewelry, okay? Here take this and put your money, passport, credit cards in side." I took what he handed me and checked it out, nothing fancy it was a travel bag that went under your clothes and around your waist. I packed it with what he told me and put it with my new clothes. At the last minute I put in our last shot, I didn't know what else, to do with it. Then I returned to the room and was ready to eat.

How is the food going? I'm starved." I really was, if I kept hanging with him I was going to lose my curves and who wanted a boy's body?

"Julie, grab that wine and go sit down on the patio, I will be right out." I did what I was told and watched the boat traffic in the Biscayne Bay. It was a nice night, the temperature was just right, with a light breeze off the water. We ate and enjoyed each other's company. That night I must have been really tired because after the wine I fell asleep. The next morning I woke up in a fluffy white bed full of pillows. I stayed they're enjoying the comfort of the warmth and the breathing of the man next to me.

******

WASHINGTON DC

The commander and Sheri arrived at the hotel in separate taxis from the airport and checked into their hotel rooms. Their accommodations had been booked next door to each other. Soon their room doors closed, the one that separated the rooms was opened and both stood looking at one another.

“How are you, Commander? Sheri smiled as she moved into his room.

“Fine, real fine,” he said. He knew he felt strange, being alone in a hotel room with a beautiful, woman. But she was at ease as she checked out his room. He watched as she pushed her long hair off her face and took a seat on the small pullout sofa, preparing herself for what was to come.

“We should get something to eat.” He motioned to the hotel menu on the table. “Get anything you want.”

“You didn’t want to go out?” Sheri asked.

“I don’t think it would be a good idea for us to be seen together. I’m just thinking about your safety, I’m not sure what we are up against and they already know who I am. I don’t want anything to lead to you,” he said.

“Okay, how about I have a salad and some chicken fingers with honey mustard sauce. Could you also get a pitcher of Ice tea? Just knock on my door when the food gets here, I am going to go and unpack and take a shower.” He watched as she moved across the room, checking out her perfect legs attached to her perfect body as she went into the room next door.

“Sounds good, see you in a few,” he waited as she closed the door. This was going to be nice to have some company, someone to reflect off of. He had always had good judgment, but sometimes you needed someone else’s eyes to see things you might have missed.

During dinner he wanted to explain about the place they were going the next night. She was young and he wanted her to be prepared for what the situation would be at this place. He hadn’t been prepared when he had gone and he didn’t want her to feel the shock that he did at first when he walked into the back rooms.

"There are a few things that I want to tell you about the place we are going to go tomorrow night. I don't want you to freak out but it is some kind of swing club." He watched her face for her reaction, hoping she wouldn't back out. She sat for a moment taking it in, thinking before she spoke.

"I didn't sign on to sleep with anyone," she whispered. I hope that isn't what you have in mind!" She looked up at him waiting for his response.

"No, no…not at all." He pulled the photo of the tan man out of a folder. "This is the man that you will need to find, he might be involved and I need to know who he is." She took the picture and looked at it, the man in the photo was okay looking, but searching his eyes she found no kindness there. The photo was a blown up picture off a driver's license, so maybe she just wasn't seeing it correctly.

Sheri just had a feeling that underneath his good looks was an evil man.

"He looks conservative, you sure he will be at this kind of place?" Sheri asked.

"Yes, I think he is the leader of this project, that I was assigned to, the other man doesn't seem smart enough to be the leader. I could be just guessing but the night I was at the club, he also used a fake name." He handed her a gray haired man's photo, this one I was able to identify from his fingerprints that I lifted from the club last time I was there." Sheri studied the photo.

"Your right, this man couldn't be in charge, I can't put my finger on why I think that from just a picture but I agree with you. You go to these places often?" She wanted to know what kind of man she was working with. There are lots of weirdo's out there, she didn't think the commander was one of them, but her judgment had been wrong in the past, when it came to men.

"No, not at all, this man from the government had me meet him there and he gave me a fake name, so I checked it out. I found that these two men were fake, besides the false ID they sent me, they were the only phony ones at the club that night. I was called again to meet this Frank guy at the club tomorrow night. I need to know what they are really up to. I have orders from up top to do what ever this Frank guy requests, but it feels funny, something isn't right. That is why I need your help. Did you bring your sister's Id?"

"Yes sir, I did as you asked," Sheri said.

"I thought it would be better in case you are looked up, that way the person they find isn't in the military. If I can break in the club's computer, so can they," he said, putting the pictures back in the folder.

"That was a good idea. Is it still okay that I do some sight seeing tomorrow during the day?" She asked smiling, "I have never been to Washington and would like to take advantage of the time."

"Yes enjoy yourself, let's say we will have dinner here tomorrow night before we go. Does that sound okay with you?" He asked.

"Yes sir, I will see you tomorrow night." She got out of the chair to go back to her room, in the doorway he called out to her.

"Sheri, please be careful and watch your surroundings." He smiled at her and wondered what it would be like to have someone like her care for him. It had never been easy for him when it came to women. He had just focused more on work, not that he wasn't interested. The women that he was attracted to were ladies that just didn't like him. He wasn't a bad looking guy; he just didn't know how to talk, to women. He was too serious and the carefree, funny men were the ones that landed the hot chicks, even if they didn't have his looks.

"Good night sir," Sheri said, as she moved through the doors separating the two rooms. He heard the door being bolted from the other side and he moved over to the sideboard where he poured himself a large dose of liquor.

CHAPTER EIGHT

The plane ride had been long, I had tried to sleep to be ready and on my feet when I arrived in Brazil. I had done my best but the excitement of going to this country had kept me awake. It had always been on my list of the top ten places to visit and now I was on my way. Quinn was knocked out most of the trip, softly snoring next to me as I tried to read my book. Damn him, always relaxed. We had just landed and I nudged him awake, he smiled. Why did he have to be so cute, even when sleeping?

Sao Paulo was the biggest city in Brazil with a population of about 20 million. Every day a person is kidnapped and ransomed for money, their ears cut off and sent to their family's, with proof of life. Because of the crime and the traffic, fleets of helicopters transport many of the rich and important businessmen on the rooftops. It is too dangerous to ride in a car where they could get robbed or kidnapped. Some people drive bulletproof cars that cost more than a home. This city is where all the very rich live right beside the very poor.

At the airport we were taken to a holding room with glass windows that held all people, from our flight. It looked like we were all flying into Rio de Janeiro. We waited about an hour and were loaded on to a different plane and off we went. It was only a one-hour flight, two hours later we were through customs and got in a cab. Quinn handed the driver the name of the place we were going. Both of us didn't understand Portuguese and had to trust that the driver would get us to were we needed to go. Quinn some how communicated the price up front in American dollars, that way the driver just didn't drive around trying to get a larger fare. American dollars were worth so much more than the Rio; the exchange was 3 Rios to 1 dollar. $100 dollars spent like $300 in Brazil.

We arrived at a high-rise south of the city, about six blocks from Copacabana, Beach. The beach was so vast, the biggest that I had ever seen, hundreds of people moved on the large sidewalk that went along the shore. Some were running or walking their dogs or sitting on benches. Small huts lined the sidewalks selling fresh coconut milk where a hole was hammered in the coconut and a straw was put inside to taste the cool nectar. There were thousands of people basking in the sun on towels where they had dug out a place in the hot sand. Children were running in the surf as there parents watched from the shore. Many fathers were alone with their kids at the beach, newborn babies bouncing on their hips as they walked in the surf. It was a beautiful place; I felt as if it was a different world. From the beach you crossed an eight—lane avenue, to where all the hotels, lined the road. Behind them rose the mountains that framed the water paradise covered with small houses stacked on top of each reaching to the sky. On one of the mountain peaks rested the Christ statue, he spread his arms wide as he protected the city.

Our one bedroom condo looked over the water; it had its own small pool with a hot tub, off to the side. I had wanted to stay at the Marriott but Quinn thought this would be better, he was right and it was a third of the price. This was so fun, I felt so happy, and I almost forgot why we were here. The country had a way of transforming your mood, making you feel far away from your troubles.

"Well you have been quiet for a long while, what do you think?" He asked, grinning like he could tell what I was thinking.

"It is the best place I think I have ever been and I just got here. What are we doing first?" I asked, thinking of what I was going to wear depending on the place we would be going.

"I have to call a friend of mine that I met last time I was here. He will be a big help, we are going to need him, and he also speaks four languages. He will be our tour guide; he can be trusted and is a good man. Walber lives in Santa Cruz, which is a little drive so I will call him to see if he can meet us tonight."

"What kind of place are we going to eat at now?"

"Just shorts and a top, beach attire," he said, reading my thoughts.

"Give me about 15 minutes and I will be ready," I said moving to the bathroom. I knew he was thinking that I couldn't be ready in that amount of time. So he was surprised when I came out quickly and he hadn't even showered. "Come on, get a move on, I want to see the city." I said as I pushed him, toward the bedroom door.

"ALL RIGHT," he said moving into the bathroom. About forty minutes later, we were at this place called the Stop and Go. It was jammed with people and the tables were really close together. No one spoke English and I felt in my own little world with Quinn. What I learned was you paid one price and side dishes of onion rings, Mac and cheese, everything, was brought to the table. We went to the salad bar and it was full of a variety of seafood and sushi. Men walked around the room with various meats on skewers. Quinn told me that the coaster that my water was sitting on had to be flipped. I looked down and one side was green for go, other side was red for stop. I got it, if I didn't want what they had when they came to the table; I flipped the card to red. This was wild and exciting.

We left full and decided to walk back to the high rise. The day was sun-drenched, and full of love of life. We passed couples on benches in passionate embraces that in the US; people would suggest they should be getting a room. They didn't know what was going on outside their cuddle. People walked their dogs, purer breeds than you saw in the US on the street, their hair fluffed and groomed wearing their sparkled studded collars.

We returned to find a message blinking on the phone. Walbert would come 9pm, we would go to a club and talk. I had about five hours to nap before getting ready for the night, I moved to the bedroom to get some rest.

"I'm going to catnap, you want to join me?"

"I'll be in later, I want to do a few things before tonight, go ahead relax." The hours passed quickly, now I hurried to get ready. Quinn had showered while I rested and was in the living room having a cocktail. The drink looked great, he told me that it was native to the country made with smashed limes and sugar with 51% alcohol. I tasted it, he told me that it mellows as the ice melts but drink it slow it will kick your ass. I took mine in the bedroom, as I got ready. I washed and blew my hair out straight and put on some light make-up. My skin always had a golden tan from years of the tanning bed. A day walking around in the sun and my tan was back. I put on my new white dress, the low cut top fit like a glove and the bottom flowed out and moved as I walked. The transparent silk, slightly showed through, were you could see my white g-string underneath. It looked nice, sexy, but in a good way. The crystals on my silver high heal sandals looked just right. I put on a crystal necklace with matching earrings, the necklace hung low in-between my small breasts. Damn, I looked better than I had in a very long time. I moved out of the room at the same time I heard a knock at the door. Quinn went to open it and he saw me out of the corner of his eye and did a double take. Ha, I knew I looked good, crazy what a little make-up and a dress will do.

His friend came in the entrance, He was about 5'10, and a blond haired guy about 35, he had a nice face, and was good looking. He looked like he could be my brother because of his coloring. He didn't look like the typical Brazilian man who had darker curly hair and brown eyes. I stepped forward as Quinn introduced me.

"This is Julie, a friend of mine." I guess that certified that I was looking good? He had to clarify that we were only friends. The man stepped forward; his arms open for an embrace. I liked him right away.

"Hi I'm Walber," he smiled, "don't mind me saying you have beautiful eyes."

"Well thank you, but yours are almost the same color," I said.

"In Brazil you see a lot more brown eyes, so when your see light eyes you have to stop and look. I am the only one out of seven brothers and sisters that look likes me, everyone looks different and we all have the same parents. Our country is so mixed with all kinds of combinations of people: Blacks, Chinese, Indians, and German. I must have gotten most of the German."

"Well I just love your country already," I said looking at Quinn; I had been so tied up talking to this man, I had to look to see if he was still in the room. I had always loved to learn about different people and cultures.

"Are you guys ready to go? Walbert asked.

"Yes, hold on a minute," Quinn took out money for the night and put everything back into the small wall safe.

"Julie, leave everything here, I have the cash that is all we need." I put my whole bag in the safe and carried just my lip-gloss in my hand.

I was ready. We went downstairs and got into Walber's small compact car and off we went.

"I was going to take you to this men's club tonight Quinn, but we can't go there because you have a lady friend. They don't let any women in unless they work there. But I know a place where we can talk and watch people," Walber said.

"That's a good idea," Quinn said. I could tell that he was hoping I didn't understand the kind of place Walber was talking about. I just let it pass and filed it away. We pulled into a parking spot and walked a few blocks to an outdoor café with seating in front, of a club. There were lots of tables full of people, most of them good-looking women. We ordered drinks and here was the lime drink again, tasty, I was starting to feel its effect. While Quinn talked about finding the lab with Walber and showing him the piece of cardboard, I was caught up watching all the people come and go as they walked along the street facing the ocean.

Groups of them would come and get a table, if it was a table with mostly men, the good-looking Brazilian women would join them. In a fog a few drinks later, I figured out what was happening. These girls were prostitutes picking up johns for the night. I had forgotten reading that prostitution was legal in Brazil, no wonder there were so many businessmen in suits. I looked around and saw some of the women looking over at my table, they were checking out the men I was hanging out with. Those two were so involved in their planning that they didn't see or care that these women were closing in. I put my arm around Quinn's large shoulders and smiled at Walber, making sure they knew who I was with that night.

"Is what I think happening here in my head or is it really happening? I asked, I stroked Quinn's arm and got distracted by a piece of his hair and put my hand up to touch it. He just looked at me with a grin.

"I think we are going to make a early night of it Walber." He made a move to stand pulling me with him. My feet didn't want to move and Quinn picked me up, put me over his shoulder and carried me down the street to the car. All I could think was that my dress was flowing in the breeze and my ass was cold and I didn't even care. Time went by fast and we were soon back at the condo.

"We will see you in the morning around 11am." Quinn said as Walber laughed and pulled the car away from the curb.

"Have fun tonight, I sure wish I was in your place!" Walber said, as he bumped the curb, driving away. Back inside of our little place, I felt hot and sat down in a chair by the pool.

"How are you doing?" He went to his knees and started to unbuckle one of my shoes, and then he rubbed, my foot. It felt so good, I wasn't used to walking in high shoes anymore. I closed my eyes and felt him take off the other and give it the same treatment. I took off my necklace and earrings and laid them on the side table, with my lip-gloss that was still tight in my palm. I stood and pulled my pretty dress over my head, folded it and put it on the chair. I stood only in my g-string and looked down at Quinn still sitting at my feet. His eyes were intense; I ran my hand through his hair; it felt so soft on my fingertips.

"Come for a swim," I said, not looking away from him as I backed into the water. I had turned my back to him as I entered the deeper water and heard him come in behind me. I twisted around and threw myself into Quinn's arms and found his lips, kissing him hard, drowning in his scent. I pushed my naked chest against his and wouldn't let go. I couldn't stop, I wanted him like no other, I just clung to him, and there was nothing but just the two of us in this little world. Time stood still, I felt him slowly pull back, the cool water replacing the heated area between our bodies.

"Julie you know I want to, I am a man, it is hard to resist you. I have to stop; please can we leave it like it is between us. It has only been seven months since her death and being in Brazil brings it all back. With my job I can't have attachments, they end up dead and I won't let that happen to you." I had sobered up at the tone of his voice. He sounded really sad.

"I understand, but after this week of being with you, I have come to care for you a little and I know you feel the same. I don't see the difference if it happens now or later. It is going to happen. With that I left the room.

******

In his room the Commander hadn't heard any noise from the space next door. He waited for a sound to let him know of Sheri's return. Not that he had his ear to the wall, but he had kept everything turned down so he would know when she arrived. He stocked it up to him feeling responsible for her, but knew he was fooling himself. She intrigued him.

The shower had stopped about 45 minutes earlier and then nothing; he was starting to wonder if everything was all right. Then a strong knock rattled the door and it swings open. All he could do was stare at her, he tried to regain some form of speech, but the words were lost as he looked at her.

Sheri was so attractive much more than he had thought, she could have been a model, walking off the front of a fashion magazine. Her long hair had been let down and curled with large rollers; it all most touched her waist. She had an olive complexion, which contrasted with the light blue top that clung to her body. Her make-up was straight off the pages of a Victoria Secrets catalog, soft light pinks enhanced her skin and the long lashes surrounding her dark eyes. Sheri was wearing a short leather skirt, and with the tall heels and her long legs the skirt was very short. He tried not to stare but he found himself gauging how many inches it was from…He moved his eyes upward studying her, he thought she was a total package of perfection; no one that he had ever seen in real life had been so beautiful.

"Sorry to stare, but you…do look lovely," he said, breaking out of his trance.

"Are you sure? I had a hard time deciding which outfit to wear. I am just a little nervous," she said, looking down and smoothing the fabric of her top.

"You look perfect, sexy and classy at the same time. With those legs, you will draw a lot of attention tonight. Don't worry, I will always be close by." She moved across the room with grace, balancing perfectly on the tall heels taking a seat across from him, crossing her long legs with grace, so everything was covered.

"What do we have here?" she smiled at him with those perfect teeth.

"Go ahead and eat, then we will prepare to go."

Sheri looked over at the pile of chicken fingers and reached over and popped one in her mouth, chewing slowly, tasting the fried delight. She didn't have much of an appetite tonight, she keep thinking of what was expected, hoping she could pull this job off, not wanting to disappoint, the commander. She watched as he walked around organizing, waiting for her to say when she was ready to leave. He sat a couple of bottles of alcohol on the table.

"What do you prefer, vodka or rum?

"I'll take the vodka if you don't mind," she said, putting the bottle, in her big bag. "Are we ready?" Sheri asked, standing.

"Yes, here is the address, I will meet you there. Now go out through your room. You will do fine, see you soon." He opened the connecting doors for her and patted her on the shoulder. In return she put her hand on his arm, for a moment pausing in the doorway, before moving out the entrance.

Minutes latter the commander's taxi dropped him at the front of the club. He tried to wrap his nerves together putting them deep down inside him, the curtain was pulled back and he moved into the large room of the club. Motion could be seen already on the dance floor, loud music banged making his heart join its beat. He went to the bar for a drink and scanned the room for her. Sheri was standing with a drink in her hand leaning against a pole watching the dance floor. He looked around the room, finding the gray-haired Frank sitting at the same table. Slowly he took in the people around the room, this time he had a purpose. Then bingo, the tan man with republican hair was standing in the shadows watching the room as if looking for attention. He had a plate of food in his hand, the commander watched as the man looked at everyone around him. He was glad that the man was here tonight proving that his instincts were right on point, he wasn't totally sure he was involved, but at least they would have a chance to find out. He was much better looking in person, his fine clothes adding to the picture of confidence. A vibe of "I'm important" sweated from his pores. He was watching Frank at the table, his head turned as Sheri took the dance floor. She had picked him out too, good girl. Both of our eyes were on her as she moved slowly to the beat, running her hand down the length of her body. It was very suggestive, and many people, men and women alike were watching her wanting to approach, with dreams of the night ahead. She acted as if she didn't see any of them, her eyes staring into the distance, then her gaze landed on the tan man. He moved forward like a bug drawn to the light, rushing over quickly as if to reach her before anyone else got up the nerve to approach.

Sheri danced up close to his body, without touching him. He would try to get closer and she would dance away and then come back in his space, toying with him, making him work for his chance. The spell had been cast. The commanders feet were in motion moving to table number five.

"Frank, How are you tonight?"

"Nick Sanson, good of you to come." He made a move to stand when the Commander didn't sit down.

"I thought that we would get right to business tonight, I have a early flight in the morning." The commander started walking toward the inside of the club, Frank followed adjusting and smoothing his clothes as he walked, his head turning side to side taking in the women walking by him.

"Yes, no problem, I have other things I wanted to do...tonight also," Frank said, smiling that lusty look that made a normal person think to keep him away from their kids, just in case. They moved to the back room where Sheri was already undressing with the tan man. She left her black underwear and bra on and wrapped the white towel around her small waist. She had a great body; he was trying not to look but like every man in the room, his eyes looked her over. The tan man nodded to Frank and left the room pulling Sheri behind him by the hand. The Commander hurried and put his things in a locker, this time he left his underwear on and wrapped a towel around his fit body. He watched as Frank struggled to make the towel reach around his white mass of a stomach. When he was finished, they moved out of the room toward the red door.

"You must be getting used to this kind of club, you're more into it tonight," Frank said, leading the way to the bar inside the back areas of the club.

"I just know what to expect, so it is no big deal," the commander said, he had, protecting Sheri on his mind and he wasn't going to let anyone have their way with her. But he didn't know what he could do, if it got out of hand, he didn't want to blow her cover tonight.

"Lets go, are you ready," he said moving down the long hall in search of a room for them to talk, Frank followed, looking in the occupied quarters they passed.

Inside an empty space with the door closed, Frank pulled out another folder and handed it to the Commander. He took the folder containing a stack of files on about twenty solders and looked at Frank.

"What is this?" He asked.

"We need you to do the same as before, you did a good job. We just need a few more solders delivered to our lab," Frank said looking down as if there was a problem. The commander read Frank knowing something had happened, that he wasn't being told.

"What happened to the ones I had delivered last month? The commander asked, a hard edge to his voice.

"We had just a little set back, but it is all being worked out." Frank looked nervous and started smoothing his towel with his fingertips, the commander could feel something was wrong. He saw sweat drip down Frank's forehead and he wouldn't look him in the eye, he was shifting from foot, to foot, he was real nervous.

"What kind a problem sir?" He said with more force than he met to have, he thought of the women Julie Redford.

"A few have passed away. The drug didn't go well with their bodies. But some times that happens. We just have to move forward," Frank said.

"What are you talking about Frank? What Drugs are they being given?"

"I have already said more than I should have, we both have our orders and you are to deliver these people!" Frank said, anger rising. The Commander got a hold of himself, he felt danger, and he made himself calm down. He dropped his head in submission staring at the floor. Raising his eyes, he smiled.

"I know we have our orders and have to obey, I don't mean to question them. You can't help but feel something once in a while." Frank nodded thinking he understood this man; he knew he would do what he was told.

"What ever happened to that girl, did she make it?" The commander held his breath, waiting for the answer.

"Between us, she seems tougher that we thought, we are trying to find her right now. That is part of the problem, she escaped, don't worry we will find her. This is all for the greater good of our country," Frank said, looking relieved, reading the commander wrong, believing the commander was on his team.

"Yes sir, you are right. If you don't mind, I just might hang around for a while. I am going to go put this in my locker and come and check out what this place has to offer." Frank looked happy that he would stay, thinking they had a bond and there would be no problems.

"Okay, see you around, just so you know, you can go in any room and join in if the door isn't locked." The Commander nodded and left the room. Away from Frank, he let his guard down, smile removed from his face as he went to the locker room. Julie had got away and wasn't dead. He wondered what had happened and how many had died and been covered up, he felt responsible. The folder looked like it contained about twenty more solders. He had a sick feeling he had to tread lightly. He hurried to find Sheri; he was relieved when he saw her at the bar getting drinks. He checked the room and didn't see the politician, after seeing what he looked like, it was easy to understand what he did by the way he carried himself. Sheri saw the commander and nodded moving down the hall, to the room with the glass window. Inside was only the tan man lying on the bed nude, touching himself. Great that's all he wanted to see, he watched Sheri move through the door leaving it wide open. He watched through the window, of the muted room, it was lit with candles and smelled of vanilla.

He could hear the man talking to her, wanting her to get undressed. She told him that she was into watching, and enjoyed watching him, but no touching. He didn't look happy as he was used to getting what he wanted. He moved in closer to her body, ripping her towel off her, revealing her black panties. He moved his hand between her legs; she took a breath trying to stand still, trying to put the drink I his hand.

"Drink this first," she said, "I went to the trouble of waiting in line for it at the bar." She moved out of his reach, holding out the drink then placed it in his open palm as he tried to grab at her again to pull her with in his reach.

"Later," he said handing the drink back; she put them both on a ledge by the door. Sheri was jerked on the bed, by her bra strap as he tried to remove it from her body, roughly pawing at her tender breasts through the thin lace fabric. With no results he climbed on top of her spreading her legs apart, with his thigh, sucking on her neck.

In the hall the commander knew he had to help her. A women was walking by, he took her hand, in his turning her towards him. She turned putting her arm around his lean waist, snuggling up close under his arm. She looked like a wealthy housewife, diamonds in her ears and around her neck. She stroked his chest, moving her hand down his trim body, where his towel was tied.

"Lets party," he said pulling her into the room where Sheri was struggling on the bed. The lady dropped her towel and looked at him, with a look of invitation and got on the bed, for someone her age he thought her body looked pretty good. The commander positioned himself behind her, moving her closer to the tan man the next thing he knew, Sheri had rolled out from under him and the lady was going down on his equipment as he spread out on the bed. His eyes were closed, Sheri made her escape, with the glasses, pulling her towel tight around her. The man on the bed didn't even notice that she had gone. The Commander gave Sheri a head start and followed her out of the club, he reaching the curb just as Sheri's taxi was leaving.

At the hotel he knocked on her door, it took her a few moments for her to open it; she stood in her bathrobe, hair dripping on the carpet.

"Are you okay?" He asked feeling bad knowing it must have gone farther than her comfort zone. But he was so proud of her; she wasn't about to let it show that it had bothered her, she was trying hard to act like she was a strong person.

"Yes, I have washed him off of me. He is not used to hearing no, if you wouldn't have come in when you did, I could have been raped. He kept telling me that I was a tease; I was at a club to get sex and give it like everyone else. So quit playing games. Funny that he thought I had to join a sex club to be able to get sex. I have never paid for it and never will if you have to buy it then it's not worth anything," she said, sticking out her chin out with determination.

"Did you get the prints?" He asked trying to steer the subject away from what had just happened. He could tell this night had opened her eyes to how some people lived. She was trying to hide that she was upset.

"Yes I got them, I have both glasses, I wasn't sure if I had mixed them up so I took both." She handed them to him in plastic bags. He moved to the doorway where she stood and put his hand to her cheek.

"You did a good job, I'm really proud of you. I couldn't have done it with out your help. Because we can't be seen here in Washington together, when we get home, I would like to take you out to a real dinner, if you will let me." He leaned in kissing her forehead as if she was a child.

"That would be nice sir," she said, looking at him shyly.

"Hey, call me Dave, we have saw more of each other tonight than most people ever do. So between us, it doesn't have to be so formal. Now go to bed and get some rest, we leave early in the morning."

"Okay Dave, I'll see you in the morning." She smiled and left through the side door. Dave sat and thought did I just ask her out? It was unplanned he thought, he had just wanted to make her feel better and to think of something else. In his right mind he would have never had the nerve to ask her out. He didn't even have a clue how old she was. He told himself not to think about it, it was only dinner, relax.

He packed his bags for the return trip putting the tape recorder he had used to tape what Frank had said and the finger print kit in his bag along with the glasses. He would work on the prints when he got back to Florida; tonight he had other things on his mind.

CHAPTER NINE

We walked down from our condo to a restaurant that looked like a large outdoor hut, off of Ipanema Beach. Walber had told us the night before that this place was where the attractive people or real people went to the beach. Not many foreigners knew about this spot, most of them went to the part of ocean that lined the road, where all the hotels where. The place was a few blocks off the water and at 11:00am it was already crowded, with the real people of Brazil. Quinn and I found Walber at a table in the corner, where he had already ordered our food. I was glad because in a foreign country I would just put my finger on something on the menu, to order not knowing, what I was getting. The food was different, some of it was fried and tasty, I wasn't sure what it was we were eating but it was all really good.

"How are you guys?" Walber asked.

"Great, these are good," I said, holding the piece of fried something shaped in a half moon. "This is a cool place and very popular."

"This place comes with a story, do you want to hear it?" Walber asked, charming me with his smile. He was more interested in talking to me than Quinn.

"Yes please tell us," I said, smiling at him and Quinn, I really was having a great time. I watched as men with instruments struck up a tune outside the open windows and moved around the outside of the building collecting tips.

"This is the place that is said to be built on the spot of a song, "The Girl From Ipanema" was written here. It started with a group of men that would sit here and every day a girl would walk by that was so beautiful that the men were speechless. They were afraid to say a word to her and when she passed the men would then turn and look at her after she had walked by. This went on every day for a long time, and instead of talking to her they wrote a song. Some of the words described a girl "tall, tan, dark and lovely she goes walking when she passes they smile". This is a true story and if you go to the back of the building, you can see her photo on the wall," Walber said smiling full of pride for his country.

"I will be right back," I said as I moved to the back of the building, I saw the photo, just as he said, hanging in a spot of honor on the wall. Beside the picture was another photo with a sign saying it was her daughter that was the new girl from Ipanema. I returned to the table to find the two of them in a heavy conversation.

Yes, I needed to focus on finding the drugs and the people behind them, no drinks for me, tonight. It was time to do the job that we were here for; they looked up when I sat down at the table.

"What is going on?" I asked.

"Walber here thinks it is not a good idea that we go any farther looking into these drugs. He knows the factory and thinks it is too dangerous for us," Quinn had frustration in his voice. I looked and saw Walber holding the logo that Quinn had found in Miami. Walber was acting like he was really afraid.

"People that have gone anywhere near the place have just disappeared, never been seen again. The word on the street is that they have many guards and poor children have been disappearing off the roads all over. It is said that this place has been taking them and using them in experiments with drugs. The government doesn't care if the children are gone missing, because so many of them run free without families, forming gangs in the favelas," Walber said.

"What are the favelas?" I wanted to know.

"They are where the poor live. Do you remember seeing all the houses that were built into the mountains on top on each other?" He said.

"Yes, I remember."

"Well they are places that has been getting larger all the time, overtaking the hillsides, they are now run by the drug dealers. Gangs of kids live there, where they just try to get by. I know you were drinking last night but did you see the kids waiting outside the club, for people to come out? If you had been alone and not with me, you guys would have been surrounded with kids begging and selling gum or anything that you would offer them cash for." Walber looked into my eyes, seeing if I cared.

"That is really sad. Why doesn't the government go in and help those kids?" I asked, wondering how small children as old as five could make it by their selves.

"There are too many of them in this country, they would rather take them out and shoot them to get rid of them. Anyhow, the drug dealers and the police have a understanding and they are left alone. These areas are watched, very carefully by the dealers. Anyone who drives a car inside has to stop and get out and move a log out of the road to pass. By the time it is removed, the whole community knows they have visitors. There are many eyes watching, it wouldn't be safe for you to go there alone without someone they knew. For sure you would be robbed and who knows what else." He patted my hand knowing the empathy I felt for his people. "One of my sons lives there, he has a small pet store."

"Do you live there?" I asked he smiled with pride that he did not.

"No, I have a small home north of here about a hour outside of the city." We both looked up at the same time to find Quinn tapping his hand on his leg. I could tell he wanted to get to business but was trying to be cool as we talked. I put my hand on his knee and patted it, "Sorry, we are ready." I smiled, looking into his eyes.

"Okay, Well, We need to find a way to get inside the building to see if we can gather some samples. Do you have any connections with the guards?" Quinn asked, looking at Walber.

"I might know a nurse who works there. She might be able to help, but it is all about money. What could you give her, to make her risk worth helping us?" Walber said as he rubbed his temples thinking.

"How much do you think it would take?"

Quinn asked, drumming his leg.

"I think about $300 American would do it," Walber said letting out a breath. I could tell he didn't want us to do this.

"Okay $300 for her and $200 hundred for you to take us there and wait and take us back. Can we do it tonight? The sooner the better," Quinn asked, smiling at him trying to break the tension that was between them.

"You don't have to pay me, my friend," Walber said.

"Walber, I know you need the money to pay for your kids. We can't do it with out you so you will take the money. I will pay you $400 instead, it will be risky and I want to make it worth the risk to you too."

"Alright my friend, I will call you later after I call the nurse. Obrigado," he said as he got up and moved out the door.

"What does obrigado mean?" I asked Quinn.

"It means thank you," he said. I nodded; I would file that away as a new word learned. "If you say obrigada you are saying it to a women.

You change the way last letter according to which sex you are saying it to." We sat for a moment enjoying the breeze from the ocean, before moving down the street back to the condo. People traveled past us on their way to put their feet in the hot sand. Moving on the stone sidewalk path down the ocean, I watched the tanned people of Brazil. They were a happy people; so proud of they're country, carefree, as they stood in the surf. When I had thought of Brazil, I thought of a beach full of g-strings. But the only ones that wore that kind of bathing suits were the foreigners with the same idea. Everyone on the sand, young babies to old grandmothers all wore the same kind of suits. They were a three quarter, two-piece string bathing suits that looked good on some and not so good on others. Most had dark wavy hair and curvy round behinds. For men that liked women, with a round ass, this was the place. I was so glad they had my kind of body, not much on top, but a lot on the bottom. The Brazilian people, didn't care how you looked in your bathing suit, they accepted all body images. It was nice not to think of being compared to others, just to be there enjoying the sun. I took Quinn's hand in mine and strolled down the walkway in silence, absorbing the culture and the sun.

We heard from Walber that day, the plan was set for 2am. That night we parked the car on a dusty side street, about a mile from the complex; the three of us took off into the jungle. We stayed on a worn path that slowly lead through the dense forest. It was dark and we were quiet as we moved through the trees. All of us were dressed in black to blend in with the night. I had used mascara on my face to block out the refection of the moonlit sky. As we drew closer the edge of the woods, the land seemed to be more manicured, the vegetation cut back around the out skirts of the buildings. Men with large machine guns could be seen on the tops of the structure and around the perimeters, walking in teams. We counted at least eight of them moving around, guarding the building. My heart was beating, I had to remind myself you are a marine; you are a marine, a fighting machine. I kept telling myself I needed to get mad to make the fear go away, tonight it wasn't working. I looked over at Quinn; he was self-assured with confidence, as always.

My heart slowed, down a little, but not enough as we moved towards the back of the building where it was darker. In the rear we encountered one guard smoking a cigarette or at least I thought it was a cigarette. The smell of marijuana drifted out to greet us as we approached. The man didn't know what had hit him when Quinn knocked him out and dragged him into the woods gagging, tying him up. He returned and we moved slowly forward to the back door. It had clicked shut as we got rid of the guard. Quinn tried to get it open with no luck and I could see anger start to build as he made a move to get to the roof. I grabbed his arm, "Let me try," I whispered and moved to the door pulling a small bag from around my waist. After a few tries with my lock picking gear, the bolt moved back and Quinn and I entered the hallway. Walber started to move in behind us, Quinn motioned for him to go back out and handed him a business card. He looked at it and moved into the trees.

Quinn and I advanced down the elongated hall to a stairway going up through the inside of the building. For a place that dealt with the making of drugs, the place wasn't very clean. On the next floor, the light reflected off glass windows that looked into a dark lab. Quinn removed a key card from inside his clothes and ran it through the door. The green light came on and we went inside the small space. Lab tables with shinny stainless steel counters full of equipment lined the walls, big refrigerators took up all the space at the end of the room. I moved in that directions, knowing the samples were most likely inside the cool refrigerators. I pulled the heavy door open and inside was trays with rows and rows of small glass tubes.

"Quinn," I called, as he came to my side, together we started loading up the small bag with the vials, careful not to drop the delicate glass. Quickly we moved out of the room, closing the door tightly behind us and rapidly went back down the stairs to the door where we had entered the building. Quinn handed me the sack, with the vials and pushed me in the direction of the door.

"Take this and wait outside," Quinn ordered. I moved out the door and found Walber waiting in the undergrowth.

"Here, take this and go get the car quickly!" I said watching the door. Walber nodded and moved to do what he was told. I still watched the door, Where was Quinn? What was he doing? I moved to take a step towards it, when I heard a sound to the right of me. I froze as a man gripped me around the waist covering my mouth with his hand. My elbow came up as a reflex and landed him right in the nose, the sound of breaking bone could be heard, as he yelled out in surprise. I started to struggle and was hit over the head, falling into the darkness, of the night.

******

FLORIDA AIR FORCE BASE

Back at the base in Florida Commander Knocks and Sheri turned on the lights in the lab and closed the door. It was late and their side of the building had been deserted for hours, the lab was a bright room that was clean and in order. Dave took out the glasses and looked at them and moved to get the fingerprint kit out of his bag, preparing to use it on the glasses.

"Dave…Commander," Sheri stammered over his name.

"Yes what is it?" he asked, trying to keep his mind in the game as he looked into those dark eyes.

"I think we should do super glue fuming just in case the prints aren't clear. If we do the dust first, we might lose what we could get from the glasses." She moved to the glass chamber they used to do the job. "This will work better, the super glue when heated condenses and adheres to the biological materials like the oils on the fingertips. Then all we have to do is run the print under a laser light and the biological material will glow. Then we take a photo and run the print through the computer to find our man." Sheri looked at the commander for the go ahead.

He nodded his head and she moved to the machine, impressed that she had thought of what he hadn't and got out the supplies needed. She put both glasses into the middle of the space and put a large amount of the super glue in a small tin and put it on the heat plate. She closed the lid until it was sealed tightly and then started the process.

"Come with me," the commander said as he led her through the passageways to the back of the building towards his office. Once inside he watched her as she moved throughout the room looking at the books he had on his shelves and the photos he had on the walls.

"You look so young here," she said as she looked at a photo of him with his buddies, in some faraway place in the world.

"I was young, I have been in the Air Force for over thirty years," he said, feeling old looking at how young she looked. He wasn't even sure how old she really was.

"You still look good, I saw you in your towel remember, very fit," she said, bringing back the memory of her in her towel. He wished he could see that again, but back here at the base, he didn't stand a chance. Someone like her wouldn't be interested in some old guy like him. He looked up, she had asked him a question and he hadn't even heard her, so caught up in his own thoughts.

"What did you say?" He asked, seeing her cross the room to stand in front of him, a question, on her soft face.

"I said how old are you? You act like I'm some twenty-year-old that just left my parents' house. I have been in the Air Force ten years myself. How old do you think I am?" He felt her eyes on him; he raised his to meet hers.

"I am old enough to be your father," he said, looking away. "I don't want you to think that I am making a move on you."

"Why aren't you making a move on me? Is there a problem? This is something that I am not used to. You know how it is with women in the military? There is always a lot of sexual harassment. You tend to get used to it and know how to deal, with it. But you are different, respectful and I like it. I don't care how old you are, I am thirty—three." She moved her hand and touched his face, he tried to relax and stop doing the math in his head. He was twenty-one years older than her. Could this really be happening, God had looked down and given him a gift. He didn't wait or the moment would be lost, he wanted to take what she was offering. The commander put his hands around her waist and pulled her close and lowered his head for a kiss. She smelled of sunshine and flowers on a spring day. He kissed her deeply, clinging to her lean body, running his hands up and down, her backside. Keeping her tight against him, he moved to the door and turned the lock. He picked Sheri up and carried her to a back room of his office where a small twin bed was kept. He laid her gently on the bed and watched her face, as her hair spread out, over the small pillow.

"Are you sure?" He asked as he waited for the answer, hoping she wouldn't change her mind, understanding if she did. Sheri nodded and pulled him on top of her. All he could think was that they had six hours.

CHAPTER TEN

The damp smell of a foul odor woke me up as I tried to stretch my body. I was sore and my head hurt like a person that hasn't had coffee in days. I kept my eyes closed, trying to get the pain in my head under control.

The room was stuffy and hot, sweat ran down onto my face and when I touched it, the smell of blood rose to greet me. Great that mother F…broke my head open when I was knocked out. I smiled with the satisfaction that I was sure that I had broken his nose. I opened my eyes as my head cleared and found that I was in a large cage. It was very dark but I could see other cages surrounding me. To my left, I made out a large shape on the floor of a cage next to mine. Not sure we were alone, I moved to the bars to get a closer look. I could hear Quinn's breathing and see that one side of his head was covered in blood and was swelling, one of his hands was twisted and looked like it had been broken. I checked myself out feeling that that I was really stiff, but felt intact. The cages to my right held small children, some as young as five years old. The child next to me was in the corner, with his back against the outer wall, his eyes were open, watching me but not moving. I smiled, he was still, just watched. "Hi," still just watched. I slowly moved closer to his side of the cage. He didn't move, flatness shone in his eyes, he pushed himself harder against the wall. Then I remembered that he wouldn't speak English. He pointed to my face and I recalled the back mascara that I had smeared all over it. I know I must have really looked a sight. I licked one of my fingers and wiped a small area off my face and his eyes lit up. I could tell he thought it was funny. Other children were watching, one said something in Portuguese and they all responded by moving to the back of their cages and didn't shift as the door squeaked open. A nurse came in and I saw the kids relax a little. She was pleasant and I could tell by the children's reaction that she wasn't to be feared. She moved from cage to cage, giving the children shots and a reward of some kind of candy she pulled from under her clothes. When she got to my cage, she pretended to give me a shot leaving my door unlocked. The nurse moved on to Quinn's cage and did the same thing; he stirred as she left, raising his head.

"Are you hurt?" He whispered. I shook my head no and moved closer to the bars separating us.

"What are we going to do? You saw what she did for us right? I think those shots we were given are still working. I don't feel as bad as I should. What about you?" Before he could answer, I heard a noise and jumped as the door to the room swung open and a woman surrounded by men with big guns came inside. She had long dark hair that flowed behind her as she approached, an evil grin on her lips.

She was good—looking, with the features that most Brazilian women had but there was something about her I didn't like.

"Well look who we have here?" She said, moving to our cages. I looked over at Quinn, seeing if he was going to say anything to this attractive, wicked woman. All I saw was his head bowed to the ground. I stepped up to the front of my cage and stared her down. She looked at me as if I was nothing, all her concentration on Quinn. His head came up and he focused on the women not believing what he was seeing, anger flashed, hurt was in his voice, as he tried to understand what was going on front of him. "Nicole…?" He stammered.

"Well now you know, I wondered how long it would take you to find out." I was watching the two of them interact, and then it came to me, oh shit. This was the woman that Quinn had been seeing, that he had thought was died. This wasn't going to be good.

"Why? Why did you do this to me? He asked softly. I held my breath waiting for the answer, hearing the pain in his voice. She put her hand in the cage and reached to touch his face, he jerked back out of her grasp.

"Come on, you were using me for your government to get information. I just was giving you the wrong information. Many people are poor in my country and if men from your country want to give us weapons and money for development of drugs, what else can I do?

These drugs can be sold for a very high price; it goes to whoever wants to pay us the most. We have come up with something that makes a person faster and stronger; the drug enhances the sensory system in the body. You of all people know how it works; you have been given the drugs. How do you feel? This can make any soldier or athlete, almost unstoppable. I have read your file, Mr. CIA guy; it wouldn't be hard for you, to join us. Your government hasn't always had your back, and done the right things when it came to you. Why do you care so much, when they don't care what happens to you? Come on, it could be like old times." She moved in closer, trying to convince him of her cause, trying to get him to look at her.

I felt his anger come out in one word "NO!" and he turned his back on her and moved to the back of his cell, no longer listening to anything she had to say.

"To bad! You will change your mind after you are in there for a while. You will beg to come back to my bed." With that, she stomped out of the room her soldiers following close behind. I looked over at Quinn as the door slammed, he was laying on his side saying nothing.

"Quinn, I am so sorry." He didn't move. "Quinn, please talk to me, we can deal with her later, we have to leave. She didn't see that our doors aren't locked." His head came up and he started checking himself to see if everything was working and nothing broken. His hand that had once looked broke was now moving, it looked stiff, but moving. For some reason he wouldn't look me in the eye.

"I'm ready," he said as he moved to stand, I did too. I handed him the sharp knife that the nurse had left. The cage door opened with ease and I looked to the left where the children where watching us. I put my finger to my lips and ran to the keys hanging on the side of the door. Running to the kid's cages, I found the one that fit the lock and pushed the doors open. I motioned for them to come out, they just looked at me and then looked at the boy that looked the oldest, he nodded and they came out of their cages. There were three of them; one looked about five and the others were about ten years old. Their clothes were worn and ripped; their bodies and hair were covered with mud. I took the youngest child's hand and we put the kids in the middle of us and moved down the hall with Quinn taking the rear. We came to the stairs and moved up to the next floor. One of the small boys pointed to the right and we all moved that way down the hall until we came to a door that led to the outside. We all ran into the woods, jumping over logs and dead brush. The kids were very fast, running as if their lives depended on it.

The shots must have been working for them also. I hoped they had not been given too much, because of their small size.

None of us were out of breath as we ran through the trees; branches scraping our skin and, tangling in my hair as some was pulled out and left behind in the undergrowth. We came out of the woods on a small road, the dirt packed tight, we sprinted across and onto the path that ran parallel to the dark street. Running full force, we jogged along on the trail that was well hidden in the undergrowth. Before we knew what was happening, a large truck was bouncing fast towards us over the potholes, of the dirt road, causing dust to fill the air. Choking with dirt in our throats, we all dove into the dense trees and laid flat on the ground, not moving until the headlights of the truck were a distant flicker. Instead of traveling on the road, we stayed on the small path, are movement was slower but we felt safer, in the cover of the trees. The younger child was getting tired, his grip on my hand had become lighter; I looked down at him and thought he looked frail. His little legs weren't as long and he had to pump his limbs twice to our one. His eyes showed his determination to get as far away as possible from the place that had held him. I wondered how long those kids had been held and shot with drugs. Quinn noticed that he was struggling and put him over his strong shoulder and we continued on. We came to the spot where we had left the car, I couldn't believe it when Walber pulled in front of us with the headlights turned off and told us all to get in.

"Hurry, they are coming back around, we have just a few minutes to get by before they see us," Walber shouted, we all piled in the small car and flattened ourselves in the back seat, pushing the kids to the floor boards. He drove fast over the tops of grass and dirt, bouncing in the air before hitting the road at top speed. Soon traffic surrounded us as we came to a main road, streetlights enhanced the tourist strip in the front of the hotels. I felt safe for the first time since we went off into the night, we had gotten away.

I looked over at Quinn holding the small boy in his lap, his large frame crushed into the back seat of the small compact car. He was still avoiding looking at me, his eyes dazed, watching out the window or pretending to look into the darkness, outside. I wanted him to be all right, things to stay the same, but what had happened with Nicole, wasn't something that he could shake off that easy. I wanted to help him, but I didn't know how. Walber broke the silence.

"What took so long? I was waiting for over three hours. I finally got through to my friend Roberta, the nurse, and she told me you wouldn't be long." Walber spoke quickly as he drove and I had to strain to understand what he was saying, his accent was enhanced. He drove in and out making sure that we weren't being followed. He said something to the kids and found that they had places to stay in the favila. He found out that men in a black van had come and snatched them just outside, as they made their way, to the beach. Walber turned the car and we moved up a windy street taking us up hill to the favilas. It was now starting to get light outside as we made our way through many turns into the heart of the favila, small houses built in close on the narrow streets, just having room to allow for the small car to have passage.

Walber got out and moved one of the many logs in the road to let us pass. No one was on the street as he pulled the car to the side of the road. The kids got out and we followed Walber to a tiny bar that was just big enough for a small counter with a foosball table in front of it. The man inside made us one of those lime drinks and Walber put in a call to find someone to come get the kids. A few people wondered in to get a look at us, not saying anything, just looking. I'm sure they didn't see many people that looked like Quinn with his size and me with my blond hair.

Many of the people that lived here never left the favila, doing all their shopping in the small stores that lined the main street. Today it was to early and the steel doors were still pulled down, not open for business at this time of day. Most of the stores were as big as my closet at home; their front doors were the width of the whole place, bars rolled down at the end of the night locking in the goods that were for sale. We said our goodbyes to the kids and moved down a narrow pathway. Small sidewalks ran in between the undersize buildings, the water in-between drained along the dark bricks, reflecting gloomy light from the shadows, between the structures making it a scary walk, if I had been alone.

Walber wanted to check on his son before we left the area. At the end of the alleyway, we found a small door that lead up, stairs stopped at a landing that was open on top of a building. To the side, little enclosed rooms damaged by the sun and overuse formed the rundown walls that were dirty and full of holes. Unclean worn furniture filled the small warm space; it was already getting hot as the sun rose higher in the sky. It smelled of old food and pets with just fans to blow the stale air around inside. I thought how fortunate we were as Americans, almost embarrassed by all that we had and took so for granted. I was ready to go and waited quietly as Walber said hello to his son. I was tired and happy when we finally made it back to our condo. When the door closed, Quinn and I were alone for the first time in many hours. I sat down and watched I waited to see if he was going to say anything about what had happened that night. I just waited as the silence surrounded us making it uncomfortable.

"Julie, I have to go get these in the mail, sending them to the lab in Florida. Did you want to come with me?" He asked, holding up the bag of vials that we had taken. I could tell that he was still avoiding my eyes;

it was starting to bother me. It wasn't fair, but for now I wouldn't bring it up.

"That sounds good, just let me shower and change real quick." I got up and went into the bathroom. In the doorway I heard a soft "thanks," I turned and Quinn was gone.

******

Washington DC

Outside the Oasis club it was 4am time to leave for the night. The tan man looked around the parking lot making sure that no one recognized him and found Frank standing on the curb waiting for his car to be pulled up.

"Frank!" he called.

Frank heard his name, turned to wait for his approach.

"Hey, how is it going, I bet you had a good time.

I saw that dark beauty that you had on your arm." He gave him a nasty smirk, full of lust. "Great, it was just great," he said, not letting on that she had run away from him.

"By the way, how did it go with our friend? Is all good?" He asked, watching Frank's face closely while he answered.

"Well, at first he wanted to know what happened to the others soldiers that he had sent a month earlier. I took care of it, and told him it went as planned. Frank said, full of self-importance.

"What else did you tell him? Mr. Tan asked.

"Just that it was his duty to do what he was told," Frank said, shifting his feet, his hands in fists as he stood, not liking be questioned as if he was a child.

"That's all you said? And he got all American and went for it?"

"Yes I told him we all have to follow orders and aren't going to like them every time," Frank said.

"Okay, sounds good, here is my car, I will be talking to you soon." The tan man moved forward and got into his limo, as the door was held open. Frank looked after him wondering how come he didn't ever have to wait when he was the one that had been standing there for ten minutes. He was starting to not like the Senator, wishing he had never taken his money and gotten involved in this box of crazy greed for power. Well, it was to late now, putting it aside in his mind, he thought of the fun he had this evening.

As soon as the tan man was in the car he pulled out his cell phone. It rang three times and a voice could be heard on the other end.

"It is time, check your post office box tomorrow," he said and hung up the phone.

******

FLORIDA

The last seven hours had been the most pleasant that the commander could remember for years. The young women that lay beside him smiled and sat up pulling him along with her.

"We don't have much time, lets go see what kind of prints we got." They both dressed and quickly went down the hall to the lab. When the prints were put under the laser lights, they shone through on both glasses. Photos were taken, both moved to the room where the computers were kept and they then scanned the fingerprints into the system. Five minutes later, they got a hit, out popped a match. The commander picked up the paper and saw a picture of Sheri; She looked over his shoulder and groaned.

"Damn, they are my prints," Sheri said, he could tell, she felt bad. Then he heard the printer start again and they both gathered around waiting and out popped a picture of the tan man, we had gotten a match. The man was a senator from New Jersey, a politician, now we had somewhere to start. The commander was glad that he had looked into these men; he knew that the man had to be involved.

"Come on, we have to go," Sheri said as she pulled him to the doorway. "Do you have a computer at your house? She asked.

"Yes, come on lets go." We stopped by his office first, where he put everything into the safe by his desk. As he turned out the lights, he saw the rumpled bed in the back and smiled to himself, what a great night.

A few hours later, the two of them had done all the research they could do on Michael Shipfield, the senator from New Jersey. He had a shady past, involved in a lot of scandals that had never been founded. His bank accounts had looked padded. Off shore accounts had been found, but the totals were not listed.

"Well now we know what he has been up to.

He's on the committee for advancement of military weapons and research. The money looks to be unlimited or hidden when it comes to the amount the government pays out to the military," the commander said thoughtfully, feeling dread rise in him.

"How does this tie into the soldiers that you had to send out to that lab in Georgia?" Sheri asked.

"I think they are trying to hide their actions and are testing drugs on solders to see the results, not caring what the results are. As long as their purpose is fulfilled, they don't care about how they get the results. This is all about money and power," he said thoughtfully.

"This isn't right. We have to do something to stop them or let someone know that can. What are we going to do?" Sheri said.

"I'm not sure who we can contact, I'm not sure how high up it goes and who is involved." He was trying not to freak out, whom could he trust, with this kind of information. The name came to him, Dick

Freedman. He was with the CIA and when they were young, they had served together on the same team, and he was a good man and would never be involved with anything like this. He could be trusted to help them. Sheri sat watching him as he was thinking, giving him time.

"Dick Freedman," he said.

"What are you saying? Is that someone you're sure we can trust?" Sheri wasn't sure, now that she was involved; she felt an obligation to the soldiers that had died.

"If something ever happens to me, I want you to get this to Dick Freedman with the CIA," he said as he pulled out a zip drive and downloaded the information and a note to the CIA agent telling him what was going on and where his files were. He pulled out an extra zip drive and copied a backup and handed them to her.

"Nothing is going to happen to you, you were just following orders," she said.

The commander thought to himself, she thinks I'm talking about being prosecuted for my actions. She is so young and innocent.

"Come here," he put his arm around her waist and pulled her tight against him. She came freely into his embrace, holding his head against her chest, running her fingers through his short military haircut.

"You know if anything happens, I can testify for you that you were doing what you thought to be right and following orders. You're a good man."

"Sheri you are a real blessing and I am glad that we have come together like this. It has been a long time since I have found someone so dear to me as you are." He stood and kissed her hard on the lips, passion ignited.

"Let me go freshen up and take a shower. Bathroom up stairs?" She pointed.

"Yes go on up, I will be with you shortly." He let her go and she grabbed her bag tossing the zip drives inside and went up the winding staircase. He heard her start the shower and sat drinking his drink wondering how he got this lucky after all these years.

The doorbell rang, bringing him out of his trance as he heard the shower turn off. He moved slowly to the door wondering who would be calling so early in the day. It was Sunday, kids down the street wanting to mow his lawn was his first thought. He opened it to find a tall lean man with brown hair.

"Commander Knocks?" He asked.

"Yes, what can I do for you?" he answered, noticing the bulge of a gun under his clothes.

"Can we talk for a moment?" The man pushed his way through the door walking in and looking around. He had the stance of a military man, you could read it by the way he carried himself. Dave felt something was wrong, his heart started to beat faster as his mind started to realize that danger lurking right in front of him.

"What do you want?" The commander said with a voice of authority, moving back to give himself room between him and the stranger.

"Shut the door sir." Dave did as he was told. The man had his gun out and motioned the commander to move into the computer room, pushing the hard gun into his back.

"Why are you here? What is all this about? What do you think you are doing busting in my home?" The commander 's voice rang in the air.

"I am here to do a job, just following orders sir. I know you understand orders. Someone thinks you know too much and I'm to stop the leak." The man's eyes were cold, indifferent to the job he was to perform.

The commander understood what was about to happen; he knew his life was about to end. He remembered Sheri upstairs and thought please don't make any noise! He had to warn her somehow. He raised his voice and started screaming.

"Get out of here! You don't want to kill me!" His voice rang from the room very clear. He moved behind the man, knocking a lamp to the floor where it smashed, breaking to bits, making a loud noise.

"I thought you would die honorably," the man shouted. Pushing the Commander back onto the chair and tilting his head back, he looked into his eyes, not satisfied, wondering where was the fear he liked to see. The man felt the power; he always did right before the kill. It was the god complex that made him feel he had life hanging in his hands. If he chose, he could spare the life, but he never did let anyone live. The satisfaction of taking life, feeling the supremacy was to great a rush. A thud of a silencer gunshot rang out and the commander fell back in the chair, a smile on his face as life left his body. The man frowned as he watched the look on his face, thinking something wasn't right. He had ended many lives and this wasn't the right reaction. He raced up the stairs.

In the bathroom, Sheri had stepped out of the shower when she heard the doorbell. She had started getting dressed while she listened to the murmur of voices downstairs. She cracked the door wondering who had come for a visit. The tone and the words became clear and when she heard the muffled gun shot the reality of the situation hit her. Quickly she whipped into the bathroom and gathered her things, throwing everything into her large bag. She didn't want to leave anything to say that there was someone else in the house. She looked for a place to hide and went to the closet, thinking to hide behind the clothes. She found a small access door and not having time to think, she pushed her lean body through the opening. A pile of empty shoeboxes filled the bottom of the closet. Putting her hand through the crack of the access door, she stacked them in front of the opening, hiding the entrance. She found herself in a two-foot passage, that lead into a tiny storage space that was over the master bedroom. Sheri hidden, sat in silence. Seconds later, footsteps could be heard coming up the stairs. Frozen, she didn't move closing her eyes as if by shutting them he wouldn't be able to see her. A loud noise drew her attention; opening her eyes she could see a small amount of light coming through the floor from a crack in the area of where the overhead light was hooked up in the bedroom. Noise could be heard from below, and then footsteps moving from room to room searching, looking, ripping things apart as the sound of movement drew closer. She held her breath thinking he could her heart, as it pumped hard with fright. He moved into the master bedroom. Slowly, carefully, she lay on her stomach, reaching her body across the floor to the light. She looked down the little crack into the room below, watching as the man stood looking into the dresser searching for something. She observed as he took everything out; it didn't look like he found what he was looking for because his body language said that he was really angry. She watched as he swung his arms, trashing the place, totally out of control. Sheri wondered if he had thought someone else was in the house or was he looking for the files.

She studied him trying to remember every detail; a round snake—like tattoo could be seen on the back of his neck. It looked like a

Special Forces tattoo that men used to wear years ago. Sheri remembered seeing them in photos, and asking what they were. While she was watching, he looked up at the ceiling in her direction. Sheri froze, holding her breath, not moving, waiting for him to leave the room. Soon she heard him move down the stairs and the front door closed.

CHAPTER ELEVEN

BRAZIL

That afternoon, Quinn and I lay down for a well deserved nap. We had been up all night and after mailing the samples to the lab in Miami, we had come back and had fallen asleep. A knock woke us from our slumber and Quinn pulled on some pants and went to the door looking out the window on his way seeing Walber's car parked on the street below. Walber came in looking worn out, his eyes were blood shot and his hair was all out of place, not the same person we had saw the night before. He fell into a chair, exhaustion evident, he was breathing hard and his clothes were damp with sweat.

"What is going on? What happened?" I asked handing him some bottled water, which he drank down fast, looking around.

"After I dropped you off last night I was chased into the favila where I lost my pursuers. They had guns and were shooting at my car.

"Whom are you talking about? Who chased you?" I asked dreading his answer.

"Some of the men that were guarding the lab. I spent the night hiding out with my son. We talked to some of the men that run the hill and they are angry at this place that has stolen many of their children. A gang is forming and going to the location tonight to blow up the building and kill everyone," he said out of breath.

"What part in this do you want us to play?" Quinn asked. "I had thought of shutting down the place, but the idea of killing people never crossed my mind. I just think the drugs should be destroyed."

"We need to show them the location and they will take care of it," Walber said, looking down, shifting in his chair.

"I don't know we can't be involved in killing people. It is different to defend yourself, I'm not prepared to go to a Brazilian prison," Quinn said and I nodded in agreement.

"We have to go, my son is involved and I can't let anything happen to him." Walber looked out the window, worry on his face. His son was under twenty with his whole life ahead of him. I looked at Quinn.

"It won't hurt to show them the way," I said. I felt we had gotten Walber involved and now he was asking for our help.

"Alright, what time tonight?" Quinn didn't look happy.

"Midnight," Walber said relief in his eyes, a silent thanks as he looked over at me. He stood and went to the door.

"Okay see you then," Quinn said walking him outside. After the door closed we were silent for a moment.

"We need to pack our things now, we are going to move our gear to the Marriott, I just have a feeling." Quinn paced the room and went and got our bags. I watched him and thought about what had just happened.

"You don't think we can trust him? I thought he was someone you could count on." Quinn sat down and turned to me. Anyone can be bought in this country, if you are not rich, you are poor and will do anything to provide for and protect your family. People have to do what they have to do to get by. It is better for us to be safe and not be set up. You know they are looking for us, in the States. What if they now know we are down here and want us picked up or gotten rid of?" I looked at him thoughtfully.

"In that case, we need to assume that they know everything, even if they don't. Lets make our own plan," I said.

"You're right, we have a lot to do before tonight. Hurry, get your stuff!" We both moved into the other room, gathering our things. It didn't take too long, we were traveling light, and everything fit into two back—packs.

The day passed quickly, time well spent as we waited at the condo for Walber to arrive. We saw him pull up and went down to meet him before he could come upstairs. Our car was followed by three dark vans with tinted windows, we moved down the dirt road in the direction of the building. We parked on the side of the road in the cover of the trees and moved forward through the jungle on the path we had followed before. Our company looked dangerous, they carried big guns and knifes that could take someone's head off in one swing. They weren't as stealth as a marine would be and I found myself scared that we would be found before we reached our destination. Excitement hung in the air as we closed in on our location. The place looked different than it had the night before, it was dark, nothing moved, and dread filled my heart. Our group moved in closer, big overhead lights came on the guards surrounded us. They had been waiting for us, tipped off. In the middle was the evil bitch controlling all the guards with the flash of her hand. She seemed so content to have Quinn in her clutches that she almost ran to him. She stood right in front of him, pushing her hair behind her shoulder and ran her hand down Quinn's back and across his ass. He stiffened and didn't move, looking straight ahead, ignoring her. What had he seen in her? How could he have thought she was a person worthy of his love? She put her hand down on his flat waist and moved lower rubbing her hand against him, showing in front of her men, the power that she wielded. That was when I lost it; I couldn't sit and watch her touch him that way.

"Stop!" I screamed, and everyone stopped and looked at me. She gazed at me as if seeing me for the first time. Her face full of hatred not used to someone giving her an order. I stood tall as possible meeting her eyes, a challenge in mine, staring her down. She walked over to me and raised her arm as if to strike me, across the face. That moment all hell broke lose as I punched her in the gut and brought my fist down on the back of her head. For a moment everyone stood in silence and then motion started all around me as fighting began. The bitch grabbed my leg, pulling hard and, down I went. I kicked out and pulled my knife as I landed on top of her. I reached out and found my hand full of her hair and in an instant; I sliced through it giving her a shorter haircut. She pulled a gun from under her clothes and tried to take aim. I moved quickly to duck the perceived bullet path. The gun went flying out of her hand. Quinn was suddenly by my side, pulling me to my feet as we turned and ran fast through the trees. I heard a shout behind us.

"Catch them!!"

The bitch screamed above the noise. I heard movement in the trees and felt that we were being surrounded. We ran hard, my short legs stretching to a full extension as the pace increased, I pumped my arms harder not wanting to be over taken. I knew unless they had been given the shots they couldn't catch us. But their pace was fast so it made me wonder if her guards had been injected. We passed the area where the cars were parked and ran on. We passed over a small stream picking up my feet high as possible out of the water moving down stream hoping to cover our tracks. After about half a mile, Quinn and I came to a dirt road, where we had stashed a small car. We jumped inside keeping the lights off and drove out of the area going south to Rio. When we hit traffic, we slowed and lost ourselves in the flow moving downtown. We parked the car where we could see the condo and waited.

"So…just a question," I said as Quinn turned to listen. "WHAT IS UP WITH THE BITCH? How could you have been fooled?" It was quiet in the car as I waited for the answer. Time ticked, just when I thought he wouldn't say anything, he spoke. His voice was strained with emotion.

"She wasn't like that, she was kind and full of love for me. The thought that it was an act is a lesson I won't forget. I have been doing this kind of work for over ten years and this has never happened." He looked sad and I was sorry that I had brought it up. I wasn't sure if it was the lose of love or the fact that his pride was wounded that someone could have fooled him.

"What kind of work have you been doing? You didn't tell me you worked for the CIA before we came down here." I put my hand on his arm, trying to give him comfort but I had to know the truth.

"I have had many assignments that are off the books obtaining information for our government. Some times you have to do what you have to, to get the information, but I have never gone as far as to have a relationship with anyone. I have had to sleep with a few people, but I have never let my guard down enough to care, for someone. You have gone under cover before, you know how it works." His look was intense. I didn't want to tell him I had never had to sleep with anyone for information.

"Have you been sent to kill people?" I asked, a sick feeling in my stomach. He paused, before he said anything.

"People have been killed, but mostly in defense or as a last resort to find out what we need to know. We are fighting a battle to save American lives, to stop the threat before it becomes reality. Please don't think badly of me." I wasn't surprised at the things that happened behind the lines that the American people never knew about. It was his plea in his voice that caught my attention. I turned my head and saw the sadness, which was quickly hidden. I pulled him in my arms, kissing his check, his eyes, and his mouth. I kissed him with the need I felt to make it okay for this big man, this Viking warrior that fought for our country, but not with out the personal cost, to himself. I wanted to take his sadness away and let him know that I understood. He kissed me back with a passion that rose out of the depths deep inside him. I clung to him not wanting to let go. He got himself under control and put me back in my seat and smiled with promise.

"Sometime soon," he said as he moved a strand of my loose hair behind my ear. Ten minutes later, a dark mini van pulled up and the bitch and Walber got out with four others. One man looked angry, an American and by the looks of it, he was in charge, you could tell by how everyone jumped to action when he gave the order. You could tell that they feared him. The man was tall, lanky with brown hair; he was dressed in a black combat outfit that contrasted off his white skin. The way he moved you could tell he had to have been in the military. He ordered the others up the stairs to the condo, OUR CONDO! When no one was watching, Walber made a run for it around the side of the building and was gone before the man could lift a finger. The American waved his arm at the men "Let him go, he is of no use to us anymore." The men turned and went up the stairs. When the man had appeared, Quinn had held his breath.

"What is it? Do you know him?" I asked.

"Yes I do, he is someone that used to be a friend a long time ago, and I thought he was dead. This goes deeper, that I thought we have to get back to the states, as soon as we can. His name is Steve Smith and he is very dangerous. We have seen what we needed to see; slowly we pulled onto the road, moving down the busy street to the front door, of the Marriott where our room waited.

******

The house was soundless as Sheri moved out of her hiding spot. She had stayed in place for hours, listening for movement downstairs. After about three hours, she felt it was safe to come out. The bedroom was a mess; clothes and contents of the shelves were all over the floor. Moving over the untidiness she slowly went down the stairs to the computer room below. Rounding the corner she found the commander in a pile half off of a chair. His eyes were glassed over; blood ran down the side of his face where the bullet had gone into his head. Sheri moved forward and closed his eyes; she tried to keep herself calm as she touched him. He had been a good man and she had really liked him, but she didn't know him enough to feel his loss as hard as it would have been if she had loved him. Still the human compassion for a person losing their life took its toll on her. She pushed back the tears trying to think what she would do next. Moving to the back of the computer she took the panel off, looking for the hard drive, with a letter opener from the desk, she was able to remove the computer part. She tossed it and the Commander's keys into her bag. In case the house was being watched, Sheri went out the back door, moving across the lawn, jumping the fence to the yard next door. Three houses down the block she went around front and lay on her stomach peering down the street. No extra cars were in front of the house, the street looked deserted. Sheri walked fast on the sidewalk out of the subdivision going right toward what looked like a more populated area. Finding a gas station, she asked the attendant if she could use the phone. She didn't want to use her cell phone because she didn't want the call traced back to her. These days a public phone was hard to find. The guy behind the counter pulled out his personal phone and handed it to her. Being attractive didn't hurt when it came to people trusting you.

First she called for a taxi, and while she was waiting, she watched out the glass window as the other drivers got their gas. A sleek black Lexus pulled in the gas station, with dark tinted windows and a man got out. She watched the tall man as he started pumping his gas; he looked from side to side taking in his environment. He started walking toward the inside of the store to pay for his gas and Sheri jetted into the bathroom and cracked the door. She watched as he paid and went to his car, leaving the bathroom she went back to the window to get his license plate as he drove off. Returning to the counter, she asked the young man if that guy had paid with cash or credit. It was cash; she wasn't going to get that lucky. She smiled and asked if she could use the phone again as the taxi pulled into the station. She dialed 911 and reported a break in at the commander's address along with the license plate, of the man in the Lexis. The guy that had killed him was still in the area or he had just missed her at the house. Her heart was racing as the cab, pulled away. How had she gotten herself so involved, she wondered? Does this kind of thing happen to everyone? She answered herself with the word No.

Sheri returned to work that night, working alone she had a chance to look up Dick Freedman at the CIA and try to give him a call. She got a voice message and explained that it was important for him to call her and left her first name and Commander Knocks name along with her cell number. Moments later her cell rang and she put the phone to her ear, she wanted to listen and make sure it was really him, calling her back. She didn't want to admit, that she was feeling a little paranoid, her voice was soft as she said hello.

"Sheri?"

"Yes," she whispered. "Dick Freedman?"

"Yes that's me, what can I do to help you? What is Knocks up to, making a lady call me; I know he remembers that I am divorced now. Ha Ha, he is funny like old times having women call to mess with me," he said laughing.

"Sir, it is nothing like that," Sheri said.

"Where is Knocks?

Put the old dog on the phone, it has been too long."

"Sir, I can't do that." Her tone was flat.

"What is wrong?" he said with concern in his voice, hearing her unexcited attitude.

"Sir, I hate to be the one to tell you this but the commander is dead sir." Sheri tried not to choke up; she had to be strong to see this through.

"What are you talking about young lady?" shock in his voice. "What has happened? How did you know to call me?"

"It is hard to explain everything over the phone, he told me that if something happened to him that I should call you. I just thought he meant if charges were brought up, not if he was dead," she said.

"Okay young lady, where are you? We need to meet. I will come to you." Dick was all business used to dealing with crisis.

"Yes sir that would be the best, I am at the Eglin Air Force Base in Florida." She felt relief and would feel a lot safer once she unloaded the material that she was holding.

"Alright Sheri, how about I meet you tomorrow night at the base and we will work all this out. Don't be afraid, it will be okay." Dick

Fredman tried to be calm, making his voice soft, making sure she would meet with him tomorrow.

Yes sir, tomorrow night." She hung up the phone and returned to her duties, trying to keep busy, to keep her mind off all that had happened.

CHAPTER TWELVE

UNITED STATES

The plane landed in Miami and we hopped on a connecting flight to Orlando where a rental car was waiting at the airport. I had done my best to sleep on the long plane flight from Brazil; of course once again Quinn was dead to the world. I had started to think it was his way, to avoid talking to me, he had been pretty closed off since we boarded the plane.

We had about a two and a half hour drive to the base on the gulf coast. We had decided it was time to check out the commander. When we had arrived at the airport, Quinn had used a pay phone to call someone that he knew at the CIA and got a machine saying the man was out of town for the next few days. He had decided that we had to go see the commander that was responsible for sending us to Georgia. There was no time to gather more information. After he had seen Steve Smith in Brazil, he didn't want us to waste any time. We would go see his friend after we had talked to Commander Knocks. Driving a fast pace, the miles ticked away as we drew closer. The sun had already set an hour earlier as we approached the base after dark receiving our passes at the gate to move on inside. Lucky for us, Quinn had some kind of military ID that let us through the gate, along with directions to the building; the commander had his office in. We hoped it wasn't too late to catch him; many had already left the base for the night. We went inside to the front desk and were lead to the back of the complex to another desk with a lone officer. She was tall with brown hair in a tight bun; she looked up as we approached.

"We have someone here to see Commander Knocks," he said, as he turned and left us with the duty officer at the desk. She stood and turned to us, her hand extended toward Quinn.

"Dick Freedman?" Quinn took a step back, looking at her with a weird look on his face.

"How do you know Dick Freedman?" he asked. She looked at him and moved away, fear in her eyes, readying herself for escape. I watched as she kept backing up towards a door at the back of the room.

"Who are you?" She said, big eyes, looking at the huge man standing blocking her exit. I stepped up to the counter and put my hand out stepping in front of Quinn. I put out my hand I could see that, Quinn was scaring her. I smiled.

"Hi I'm Julie Redford, Marine. We are here to see Commander Knocks."

"Quinn Rock, sorry about that, I just know a Dick Freedman. Why did you think, that I was him?"

"He is meeting me here tonight." Just at that moment, a burley man about 5'10 walked through the door escorted by the same man who had lead us through the maze, of hallways. He saw Quinn and came in for a big bear hug.

"Quinn, it has been too long, how are you doing? Have you had about enough time off?" He said smiling; he reached over and said to the solder at the desk.

"You must be Sheri," she nodded, watching all of us. He leaned over the desk and took her hand in his and winked. "Dick Freedman CIA, at your service." He turned to me and eyed me from head to toe with a smile deep into his eyes.

"Who is this little cute thing with you, Quinn?" He asked with a sparkle that made his eyes glow, the bright blue complimenting his silver hair. I stepped in front of Quinn again and stood up taller and gave him a firm handshake.

"Julie Redford sir." I liked this man right away and could tell he was a good person; it was just a vibe that came off him. He was very easygoing, uncommon for a man is his position.

"Sir, I tried to call you today," Quinn said.

"This is your friend in the CIA?" I said looking at Quinn as he nodded.

"I just received your message on the drive here. But I had some business to take care of with my friend Sheri." Dick looked at her for the first time, she was a knockout. "Commander Knocks was a good friend of mine from before your time. He got involved in something that got him killed and I am here to find out what has happened," Dick said, sadness could be seen around the corners of his eyes as he mentioned the commander.

"I'm sorry sir, I didn't know he was a friend or I would have called you sooner. I think that we were led to him because of what he was involved in. That's why we are here to find out what he knew," Quinn said, empathy in his voice. Dick turned to Sheri.

"Sheri, is there someplace that we can all go and talk? He asked.

"Yes, just let me get a relief for my post and I will take you down to Commander Knocks office. I need to show you a few things," she said as she moved around Quinn to the phone, then around the desk leading us all down the hall. Moments later, we rounded the corner to a back hall and Sheri took out a set of keys and started trying them in the door, until she found the one that opened it. We all went in and were surrounded in paper and trash that was all over the floor, along with personal items and books.

"Someone has been here! This isn't how we had left it two days ago. How would they get on the base without clearance? Commander Knocks and I thought the orders were coming from high up but we never found the military connection. This proves it is not just political as we thought. I had been afraid to come in here earlier by myself." She looked toward the back room were the bed had been left unmade in their hurry to leave. She went over and shut the door before going to the side of the desk and pulling back the rug to reveal a floor safe. Letting out a breath of relief, she saw that they hadn't found it. Sheri calmed down and turned to the room of people.

"If you will all pull up a chair and I will tell you what has been happening here." She looked at Quinn and me. "Just to fill you in, the commander died about twenty—four hours ago at his house. I saw the man who did it, he didn't see me."

"What did he look like?" Dick asked.

"He was tall, lean, with brown hair and had a military look. "Quinn looked at me and then at Dick.

"I think I know who it is. I just saw Steve Smith in Brazil, ten hours ago," Quinn said.

"Your sure it was him?" Dick asked.

"Yes I'm sure, we used to all be friends remember? He must have faked his death after that one case in Amsterdam where those diamonds came up missing. Now we know where they must have gone."

"Did he have a round snake tattoo on his neck." Sheri asked. Quinn looked at her and nodded and pulled the back of his shirt down revealing the same tat-too on the base of his neck. She had been on the floor trying to get the safe open and nodded that it was the same, I moved down to help her. Reaching in my pocket, I pulled out my lock picking kit.

"I don't think we will need that, I have the combination right here, maybe you could try it. My hands are shaking to much to open it." I put my hand on hers and gave it a squeeze.

"Tell me one number at a time," I said as I moved the numbers slowly and popped the door open. Sheri reached in and pulled everything out and handed it to Dick.

"This is what we have. The commander was ordered to write orders and deliver different kinds of military trained solders to a lab in Georgia. He felt it was fishy and asked me to assist in getting information. Here are all the files of the solders, names and backgrounds. The fingerprints are the men that he met with in Washington, the same men that he received his orders from. We also did some background on both of them." Sheri dug in her purse and removed the computer hard drive and two zip drives. This is the information on the politician that is running things. I took the hard drive, just in case, out of the commander's computer at his home, I didn't want them to know what we knew. You don't want to know what we had to do to get all this information. I am really going to miss the commander, he was a real good man." She bit her lip looking down, trying not to show she was upset.

"Sheri, you have done a real good job, the people in this room are the only people that know, what is going on in this case. I want you to take a leave of absence and work with us. That way you won't be here alone and we could use your help, no one knows you are involved right?" Dick asked.

"I am pretty sure they don't know I was involved, we were really carful. So you're saying you are going to pay me to work for the CIA?"

She asked, a grin on her face. "How much are we getting paid?" Sheri asked.

"Yes, you will work for the CIA and how about five pay levels higher than you are getting now." Dick said, laughing at this super model worrying about money.

"That's great, in a week I was upgraded three levels and now five levels higher, eight levels in one week. I hope I stay alive to get to go shopping when this is over." She was done with all she wanted to say and watched Dick look through the files. Dick looked at me and I looked Quinn.

"Why are there files on both of you here?" Dick asked, surprise in his eyes.

"Sir, it is a very long story, but the gist of it is we were kidnapped, injected with some enhancing drugs, that improves our strength and abilities. We escaped together and found the place the drugs are being manufactured and tested on people in Brazil. This all ties in to the case that I was working in Brazil a few months ago. We never found out how the drugs were coming into the US or where they went afterwards. None of the them were ever found on any of the ships in Miami," Quinn said, looking like he was back to normal now that we were out of Brazil. He seemed excited to be working on this case, now that we were sitting here and not in a place that reminded him of the bad things that had happened in his life lately.

"Are you guys feeling okay? Do we need to get you checked out?" Dick asked, concern on his face. "I'm not ready to loose any more friends."

"We are okay, we'll get checked out after all this is over," Quinn said looking at me, to see if I agreed, I nodded my head.

"Okay kids lets see what we can do, with us all working together, I need to take all this information back to headquarters in Washington. I will get a few key people to work on digging up some more. Sheri will go with me and we will work on the politician and the money part of the drug trail." I looked over and I saw her make a face.

"What is wrong? I whispered and relaxed when she laughed.

"I didn't think I would be wearing my glass striper shoes any time soon," she said. I wondered what she was talking about, but just laughed along with her. I liked her, she was cool. I was glad, most of the time when a girl is knock dead gorgeous I've found that they were not very nice. We heard the men laughing and both of us looked in their direction.

"You get all the luck, you get to go to the strip club," Quinn said punching his friend in the arm. Sheri and I looked at each other and said at the same time,

"MEN."

"Like I was saying," Dick, said, "We will do Washington and you guys will follow and find the drugs. I hope they are still in the testing stage; we don't need them ending up on the streets in America. If what you are saying is true, people would die if they become street drugs."

"I think they are still in the testing stage and haven't been sold as of yet, but time is ticking, we sent them to a lab in Florida," I said. "By the way, I hope we are on the CIA payroll because we are about out of cash."

"I will wire you some money in Miami. Now business is done, where are we staying tonight?" Dick said looking at Sheri with those baby blue eyes. "Are you up for some houseguests?" She looked around the room at everyone looking in her direction.

"I guess we are all going to my house, I just have one guest room and a couch. I will call for carryout. Does that work for everyone?" We all nodded locking the office behind us. At the front desk, Sheri typed a form and left it with her replacement. Dick pulled out some papers out of his briefcase and signed them and put them on top of the papers Sheri had filed. Now we were a team and we had a plan.

******

Brazil

Back at the factory Steve Smith slammed the door shut on one of the cages. “How could you let them get away? You’re lucky Quinn didn’t see me, the United States government thinks that I am dead and I want to keep it that way! YOU STUPID BITCH! You said you had him under control; it was your idea to fake your death. It would have been easier for me to kill him and to get rid of him.”

“Well it worked, it got him out of the country and off of the case, he was getting to close,” Nicole said, pacing the room.

“Too close to what finding out or to winning your heart? Don’t tell me that you didn’t start to care for him just a little! All that lovey dovey you both were having!”

“It was not like that, it was only our business that I was thinking about, he didn’t get to me,” she said, putting her back to him, not letting him see her face. She had to control her feelings or she was going to get herself killed. This Steve Smith was a killer and a user, he wouldn’t think twice about offing her. She turned and came to stand in front of him wrapping her long tanned arms around his lean waist.

“You know you’re the only one for me, Quinn was nothing but useful in getting us the needed information to keep going.” He wrapped his arms around her believing what she had said. He calmed down and filtered his anger into lust, giving her a hard kiss, pulling her to the table in the middle of the room. He ripped her top off and pulled her pants down and thrust into her from behind. He moved hard and fast, pulling her hair back and squeezing her ass so hard she had to bite her lip trying not to cry out. She hadn't been ready and pain ripped through her as her entrance felt like it was torn open. She rode the wave of ruff sex. She felt his release and was happy when it was over. She wished it had been Steve she had gotten rid of instead of Quinn. He had never treated her this way; he had always been tender and kind. To good for her, the feelings that had come to the surface had been unexpected. She was told to use her body to trap him, to get what was needed, to play the part. Letting him think it was her that he was helping as she used him. Nicole had enjoyed it and for a few moments, she thought that maybe it could work. But for a person that had grown up poor, the daughter of a prostitute, not knowing whom her father was, it didn't make sense. Life had made her a fighter, a person that would do anything for the money. Like her mother, she had used her body to get what she wanted. So she had followed the cash, instead of her heart and taken what she could. Smith had said something and she looked up, watching him take the strands of her hair, out from between his fingers.

"Are you not listening to me? I said we have to get things done. This room needs to be filled up with new kids. We have almost refined the drug and know how much to give without killing too many. The scientist Belvar is working on my other plan. By using the blood from those injected, we can reverse the effects that the first drug does. Than we can control the market, having two drugs that we can sell. These will double our money. We will put a high price on them both and if our politician friends in the US government don't want to buy them both, and then we will sell it to their enemies. Trust me, they will buy at whatever price we set. They don't want anyone else to have an advantage over their country," Smith said, looking pleased with himself.

"I thought it was your country too," Nicole said.

"It isn't anymore after all that they have done to me. I am a man without a country." He was angry and she backed out of his reach just in case.

"I also have a side project going that I need Quinn and that girl's blood for. You know our politician friends had to do their own testing to see if the drug really worked before they would buy. They had a better idea and tested the drug on soldiers instead of kids to see if the reaction would be better. They were right, now I want the blood of the two soldiers that made it—Quinn and his girlfriend." He wasn't watching when Nicole cringed when he said girlfriend.

"That is why all the shipments. Soon as we sell to them we could always make a batch and sell to whoever we want, the money is unlimited," Smith said.

"What is this side deal that you made?" Nicole asked, money back on her mind. All this talk of money made her remember why she had made the decisions that she had made to stay with him.

"I made a deal with their scientist, Belvar.

He is working for me, and the United States Government. I wouldn't let him say no," Smith said, looking pleased with himself.

"The next shipment is ready in two days. I will see that it is moved to the dock and loaded aboard the ship," she said as she stood adjusting her clothes, walking a little stiff. "What about Quinn and the girl. Do you want us to keep looking for them?"

"No, we won't waste time on that. I checked with a friend at the airport in customs and found that they left the country. I have friends in the states that are looking for them now, they will be found. If they come back, I will be informed. Lets get out of here, I have plenty to do." They moved to the door and were soon thinking about the job they had to finish getting the shipment ready.

CHAPTER THIRTEEN

The next morning after the sun had came up Quinn and I left the small house. It had been a nice night talking among friends, relaxing before we left knowing of the job ahead. We had driven the car back to Orlando and flew to Miami, getting to Quinn's condo around 1pm. Quinn had called Walber who was really happy to hear from us. He had said that he hadn't been given a choice; the men had caught him that night after he had dropped us off. They had threatened his son's life if he didn't do as he was told. Quinn assured him that it was okay, but next time tell him and he would be better prepared.

Walber was "soooo sorry." I didn't know if after what had happened, we should trust him, but Quinn had said we had no other choice. He over knighted a package in care of Walber; these items wouldn't make it past customs. I listened as Quinn made things real clear to Walber.

"Just remember Walber, I also know where you family lives, don't make me come pick up the package at your house," Quinn said.

"No, no, I will be ready when you call!" I could here the stress in his voice. Quinn hung up the phone and we looked at each other.

"Do you think he will do what you asked him?" I wanted to know.

"I think he will, he feels really bad about what happened." Quinn said "But now we have lots of money to work with so if he falls through, we will not have a lot of time to find the things we are going to need."

He went to the closet and pulled out two worn leather backpacks that were a little bigger than our current ones. They looked well traveled.

"Which one do you want? Black or brown?"

"I will take the brown, it will match my outfit. Just joking, okay forget that one. What are you saying? This is all we are bringing?" I asked.

"Yes, we have to travel really light and this has to fit inside." He handed me a shorty 3mm wet suit with some black skins. Bring a bathing suit and a change of clothes you can layer," Quinn said, handing me the items along with the leather backpack.

"All I want to know is where you got this wet suit at such short notice. You just don't have extras hanging around or does the girl you date have to be able to get her ass inside this one to be called your girl." I thought these had to be someone else's but they looked new. Could a man be that organized? I could have sworn that these weren't in the closet when I was here just a few days ago.

"You're funny, now take your ass in there and pack your bag, you can put all your other stuff in the closet in that bedroom. I opened the door he had pointed to and found the space empty and waiting. I stashed everything else inside the bedroom closet as I packed my backpack. I didn't see any other women's things anywhere in the condo, meaning he didn't bring many women here or he got rid of things when the connection was finished. Our relationship had fallen into a comfortable partnership. I got along with him better that any man that I shared this much time with. I liked his mind and the easy way he laughed, the way he wanted to protect me but didn't crowd me, the way he pretended not to pay attention but listened and took in every word that was said. Well that alone was enough to draw me in, but he had one of the best bodies I had ever seen on such a large man. At 6'5 he was very well cut, like a big cat his body was powerful. He was tan and with that hair a little longer, he looked like a Viking warrior from times past. I needed to quit thinking about him; he had told me that in time something would happen with us. But how much time was he talking; I had never been with a man with so much self-control. I was wishing he didn't have so much of it; I was tired of being the aggressor. I looked up and he was in the doorway watching me, I jumped, feeling like I had been caught and he could read my mind.

"Yes, can I help you?" I said trying to cover that he had scared me. But I'm sure he saw me jump.

"Sorry, I didn't mean to frighten you, I had called your name and you didn't answer. Our carryout has arrived, and when I didn't hear you, I came looking to see if you were done. Are you ready?" He stood there staring at me.

"Yes…I'm done." I handed him my backpack; he lifted it with one arm checking the weight, looking around the room, to see if I missed anything.

"I'm starving, lets eat!" I moved to the door, waiting while he blocked my way with his big frame. He lowered his head to come in for a kiss, I moved and he caught my cheek before I went around him and skirted out of the room. New plan—make him chase me until he has to have it. If one-way isn't working use another, this was going to be fun. Dinner went by fast; I went in his room, put on my nightgown and got in bed. I was real tired from the past few days and had to get some rest the plane left at 9pm that night. An hour later, I felt him get into the bed and draw me closer to him, as I fell back to sleep.

Time passed fast and before I knew it Quinn was shaking me awake, we left for the airport 30 minutes later. Here we go back to Brazil. I couldn't believe it but I slept all the way there and felt refreshed as I brushed my teeth in the small plane bathroom. The plane taxied to our gate, Quinn called Walber and told him to come pick us up at the airport. Backpacks on, we moved to the curb as the car pulled up. Before we could open the door, Walber was out hugging Quinn.

"I am so sorry my friend, please forgive me."

"All has already been forgiven, come on lets go, and did my package arrive?" Quinn asked wanting to make sure we had what was needed.

"Yes it is in the trunk," Walber said smiling and happy that Quinn was pleased.

"Good job, Obrigado my friend," Quinn said, patting him on the shoulder as he looked back to see how I was doing in the back seat.

"Where are we going?" Walber asked.

"To your son in the favela, it will be safer for us there. At least we won't be snuck up on there, people will know if visitors are around," Quinn said.

"Your right, good idea, my son will be happy to have you."

"It will only be for a few nights and we will pay him rent. Also we will pay you for being our taxi and tour guide." Walber looked happy with the outcome. We stopped at a small store and picked up a large box of food to take up the hill. The selection was better than you could get once inside. It would make the family we were staying with very happy. Inside we passed a soccer field with kids pushing a ball around as dust flew in the air. This was a country that even with all its problems had real pride for their sports teams. They would crowd the stands on game day cheering for their favorite soccer team, dressed in the team's colors, doing prepared chants and cheers, dancing in the stands until they vibrated with motion. Soccer was started young, intertwined into the blood of the people like baseball was in the United States.

Walber parked the car and we moved through a maze of buildings that only the people who lived there knew their way around. Quinn made me walk in front of him following Walber's lead, he carried the box of food and package from the trunk. We climbed the stairs and found Walber's son inside, playing old video games on a small 12-inch TV. Roberto's sons sat watching him play the game.

"I have brought you some guests," Walber said in English and then spoke to his son in Portuguese. Roberto didn't speak English like his father and he listened and smiled at us. I took the box out of Quinn's arms and put it in Roberto's and he really smiled. Before he could walk down the narrow hall to the kitchen, I grabbed a box of cookies off the top and handed it to his boys. They jumped around as if it was Christmas, doing little dance steps; the game they had been playing was quickly forgotten.

Walber stayed with us and we had dinner with the family, he wasn't going to leave our side. He was making sure we were safe as we hid out in the favela. Time passed quickly. After the boys had gone to bed, Quinn got out the package and set it on the table. He ripped it open, pleased that it was just as he had wrapped it the day before. He reached inside and pulled out some gun parts with a lot of ammo and some big knifes, along with something rubber. I watched as he pulled out a small cylinder of mace and set it in front of me.

"What is this? I asked with a little attitude. You get guns and I get mace! Something has to be wrong with your brain!" I yelled.

"I am going to give you one of these guns after I put it together, so calm down junior agent." All right what a jerk! I moved over and grabbed the parts to the biggest gun and clicked it together and had it loaded in half a sec, slide clicked back and bullet popped out into the air right into my hand. The men at the table did look like they were impressed, I looked at Quinn, he wasn't happy.

"Tell you what, I will let you put all the guns together if you let me have that gun." I thought about it and handed it to him and he let out a sigh of relief.

"Julie, this is my gun and it has been modified to have such a hair trigger that I thought you might shoot one of us by accident." Whoops, now I felt stupid trying to prove myself.

"Sorry about that," I said looking to see if he was still mad. But he just sat calmly looking at me. Damn, he was a tranquil guy. I would have gone off if someone I was working with had pulled that.

"Come here." I did what he said and he put his arm around me pulling me close. "I just don't want anything to happen. I know how tough you are and well trained, the mace was not an insult but a gift. I thought you could hide it in your sports bra where it won't be found if you are searched and removed of your weapons."

"Thank you, that was so kind of you to think of me." I felt like I was getting teary and thought what the hell is wrong with me? I climbed into his lap and held him like I was a small child. I didn't care that the men at the table watched.

I didn't care about anything but Quinn and that moment of kindness.

The next morning we rented motorcycles and drove to the marina, where most of the larger boats were docked at the shipyard. Parking on a hill, we looked through binoculars, down into the large boat yard. Quinn knew what ship he was looking for and was happy when he found it tied down at the dock.

"Walber I need some information on that boat docked at Pier 3—lot number 323. Do you see the one I am talking about?" He handed him the binoculars and waited until he found the boat and nodded.

"What do you need to know?" He asked.

"How long has it been here and when does it leave, also if you can find out who owns it or what company it belongs to," Quinn said.

"I can find that out, wait here," he said as he swung his leg over his bike. I walked over to him. I wanted to say something to him before he left.

"Walber wait, if you have any trouble take this red bandana out of your pocket and we are on our way. Now please be careful." I reached over and gave him a kiss on the cheek. He smiled with embarrassment and took the bandana, shoved it in his pocket, and left at a fast pace not looking back.

"You are so funny. Don't be scaring our only help!" he teased. We watched as he drove down the hill to the entrance to the marina below. He talked to the guard for what seemed like a long time and drove away. At his return he parked next to us and got off the motorbike and took off his helmet, a grin on his face.

"We aren't going to have a lot of time to get ready. The boat pulls out in the morning around 6am, on its way back to Miami. It has already been loaded and is waiting for the crew to check in. They are on a different ship that is due anytime coming in from America. He wasn't sure who owned the ships but he said they make the exchange almost every month."

"Good job, Walber, you're alright, there is not a lot of time, but enough. Come on everyone let go back, we have a boat to catch early tomorrow morning." I just looked at him as if he was crazy.

"What are you talking about?" I wanted to know.

"We aren't going to be taking a airplane back to the United States," he said, pulling me on the back of his bike and I wrapped my arms tightly around him, holding on tight as we went back up the hill. We were on our way. Great, now I understood the wet suit.

******

WASHINGTON DC

After seeing Quinn and Julie off in the morning, Sheri prepared a large suitcase with all kinds of clothes to bring to Washington DC—some business, striper attire, sleep wear (not too sexy), jogging clothes. She felt like she had to be prepared for anything that came her way. Dick had been sort of funny after Quinn and Julie drove off, making jokes about the two of them. He thought something was going on between them but we had seem no evidence of it last night except them sleeping in the same bed. In the middle of the night, when Sheri had to go to the bathroom, the door was open and she looked in, they were both just sleeping, cuddled up on top of the covers. Dick was sound asleep, ten feet away on the couch, his light blue flannel pajamas budging at the seams as he twisted in the covers. It was crazy how the past few days had changed her boring go to work and home life. Sheri always knew that she had more in her, but because of her looks, she had always been put in a category, of not tough, too girly. Now was her time to prove them all wrong on that account. The pay increase was going to really help, her mother had been sick for a long time and the medical bills had been piling up. The insurance didn't cover everything and anything extra that she could make would really help.

Dick started moving around in the living room and Sheri looked to see what he was doing. She smiled to herself as he tried to look busy while he waited for her to finish getting ready. Sheri walked out, shutting the blinds and turning the temperature down, closing down the house. Sheri didn't know how long she would be gone. She pulled the big red suitcase behind her, trying to look cool as she did it, but it had to be at least 100 pounds. Dick watched for a minute and then jumped up to help.

"Here, let me get that for you." He moved over to grab the bag.

"That's okay, I got it." Sheri pulled the heavy roller bag behind her to the door, running over the end of the coffee table. She made it out front and turned to look at Dick, as if to say are you coming. Surprised he hurried up behind her.

"Can you pop the trunk?" Sheri asked, he watched as she lifted the large red suitcase and tossed it into the back of the trunk like a bag of potatoes. Sheri knew to him it might have looked like she had done it with ease, but she could feel her lower back say you forgot to bend your knees. Sheri stood up straight and lowered herself into the front seat, feeling the strain.

They drove to the airport and flew into Washington.

At the airport they picked up Dick's car, inside she wasn't sure where they were going but wasn't going to ask him, She thought she would know soon enough. They pulled into a well-established area, 30 minutes outside the city. Large massive trees surrounded the street; they grew over the road stretching their branches in the sun's direction. The area made you feel like you were in the country, far away from everything. Dick pulled up to a gate, he put in a code and they moved down a road that ended in a circle drive, in front of a large white estate, surround by out buildings. Flowers were planted carefully in organized beds with a maze of trimmed trees lining the circle. Sheri felt she wanted to just sit in the car and take in the beauty of the estate. Pillars rose to line the front of the mansion, a long overhang enclosed the whole front of the grand porch, leading to nine-foot wooden doors that slowly opened. An older women and a small child stood looking out, smiles on their faces. The little girl took off running and jumped off the stone steps, screaming at the top of her lungs.

"Daddy, Daddy."

As soon as the car door had opened the child had tossed her body into Dick's arms squealing with delight.

"Amanda, my cute little munchkin, what have you been up to?" He said as he tickled her and she wiggled out of his reach.

She whispered in his ear and Dick turned to look at Sheri.

"This is my friend Sheri," he said as the child peeked around his leg. She was a cute girl with long wavy blond hair that fell down her back. Sheri took her to be about five or six years old. She had big blue eyes like her father and a chubby cherub face.

"Hi Amanda, it is nice to meet you," Sheri said, sticking out her hand toward the small girl, she moved slowly and ran up and slapped Sheri's hand in a high five and ran back behind her father.

"You funny little girl! Can I hold you?" Sheri asked. Amanda shook her head no.

"Okay maybe later," Sheri said, faking a frown as if she was going to cry. Dick was laughing, holding her hand as she looked to see if Sheri was for real.

"She will warm up to you and when she does you will want her to go take a nap." Sheri laughed; it was nice to be around a child, it had been a long time. He turned to the lady at the door.

"Sheri, I would like you to meet Ann, the woman in my life. I looked and Ann moved forward and shook my hand. She was a woman that walked with power, Sheri could tell she was used to being in charge.

"Nice to meet you Ann," Sheri smiled at the older, striking women. She had the same kind of white gray hair that Dick did with the same light blue eyes that sparkled, as they looked her over with kindness.

"It is about time Dick brought home a lady friend," words left me for a moment and I quickly rebounded. I had thought that this was his wife but now understood this must be his mother.

"Now don't be messing with Sheri, we are working a case together, we are friends." I could see that he was a little uncomfortable.

"Yes, we are good friends, I just needed a place to stay while I am in town working a case. We thought it would be easier to stay under the same roof. I hope you don't mind." I saw relief cross his face and was quickly gone as he winked at me behind his mothers back.

"You are more than welcome, we are happy to have guests." She flowed into the house and I followed her. The entrance was so beautiful; two winding staircases lead to the top of the stairs. Old paintings of relatives from the past, hung on the walls giving a felling of old money mixed in with a new modern feel with the latest addition, to the old estate. They both came together nicely with great taste and care that had been put into the place.

"You have a wonderful home," I said looking at Ann.

"Thank you my dear, we love it too. It has been in the family for four generations, five if you count Amanda. My grandparents built the house before there were any other dwellings around. We have been happy here, there is plenty of room, for everyone and their family'.

"If you don't mind me asking, how many people live here now?" I asked.

"Just the three of us live here now, in the past the house held at least thirty, counting the servants. Today the cooks, cleaning people and child care don't stay here as they once did," Ann said. I looked over at Dick; I could tell that he didn't like talking about the help. It was a different generation and I found it all interesting. I wondered where Amanda's mom was or if she couldn't take living under the same roof as Ann. It was none of my business, but you always wondered about the people who you were staying with.

"I will show you to your room," Dick said, turning to Sheri to lead the way.

"Is the blue room okay for her or did you have something else in mind?" Dick asked his mother.

"Lets put her in the pink room, it is nicer and down closer towards the end of the hall." She said, smiling as if she had a joke. Dick knew what she was saying and rushed Sheri up the stairs towing her and her suitcase behind him away from his mother.

"She has gotten a little pushy with women after Amanda's mom and I broke up two years ago. She would be happy if I filled up the house with children, girlfriends or wives. I am an only child and Amanda is also a only child, my mother thinks we will have no one to take over the estate if I don't have some more kids," Dick lead the way down the long hall decorated with old paintings that must have cost a fortune in today's market. Sheri tried to look as she passed interested art from days past, the quality was always really good.

"I understand, don't worry about it, mothers always worry, it's because she loves you." Sheri tried to make him at ease.

"She makes me feel like a kid at this old age, like I am young again wanting to do things that would please her. The room she wants you in is my ex.'s old room right close to my bedroom." He opened the door, it was done in very tasteful pastels and in the middle was a high feathery bed with pink fluffy pillows. A window looked out onto a beautiful flower garden at the back of the house. The smell of the sweet scent of roses drifted in the window. Sheri walked over to the little nook of a window seat and saw him waiting for my approval.

"This is perfect, the best," Sheri said and meant it; she was surrounded by beauty and took a deep breath, happy that she had gotten this room.

"That isn't all of it, over here is your own bathroom. Come with me." He motioned through a door and we walked into a sitting room. It had a desk and comfortable furniture set up in front of a huge fireplace.

"Here is the reason why she wanted you in that bedroom." I watched him walk over to a door and opened it and went inside. Sheri followed Dick and was inside a very masculine large room with dark wood a hunting scene on the walls. Heavy drapes covered the windows blocking the light. The room had a woodsy scent, all male here, just like Dick.

"I see what you mean, it would be easy to do things and no one would know. I will keep that in mind, and watch myself when I am sleep walking." They laughed together, he was funny and I could tell he wanted to make sure that I felt comfortable. That, for some reason, made a difference to him.

Interesting, she thought.

"Do you want to get settled and then we will head downtown to my office, we need to get a few people working on research. Is that okay?" He was asking her permission, Dick was my new boss and she felt he was treating her as an equal.

"Yes sir, whatever you want to do, I will be ready in 15 minutes." Sheri moved to her new room taking a moment to take in the scent of flowers as she hung clothes in the closet showering real fast. She tossed her hair into a tight bun and threw on a business suit, heals, with some light makeup. She was ready. Sheri went into the middle room and saw Dick take a double take when he saw her. It is funny when men are confused when you are ready when you said you would be, but she know it wasn't the only reason he was surprised when she walked in the room.

"Is this too much for the office?" Sheri asked looking down at her high heels.

"No, you just through me off being ready so quick, let me grab a few things and I will be right with you."

"I love it, a man I can beat getting ready."

"I'm too old to move to fast. So prepare yourself for what comes next."

"What a handy capped parking sticker on your car? Your not that old."

"Very funny, young lady." Dick came back in the room ready polished with his suit jacket over his arm, straitening his tie."

Sheri put her hand on his arm and together they left the room. At the office Dick was all business, he had a higher position than she had thought, people ran around to do his bidding, as soon as they saw him entering the building. Parking in the underground garage they had taken a guarded elevator up to Dick's office. He introduced Sheri quickly as they walked by people, in no way would she remember any of their names. Sheri could tell they were wondering who she was and what she was doing in the building. Within a few minutes we were inside Dick's office and Sheri had her own CIA badge. Dick sat her in front of his computer and set her to work doing research. In the process a small team of three entered the room and Dick briefed them and sent them on their way assigning them jobs digging deeper into files that aren't available to the masses. Phone taps and surveillance teams were called in to follow our politicians. Sheri was looking up general information on the drugs and what was contained in their formula that had come from the lab in Florida. She also started pulling a file on the scientist that was in the back woods of Georgia. Doctor Belvar was a man that had, in the past, been involved with some kind of banned human cloning. He had for some time disappeared to an island in the South Pacific. When he reappeared a few years later, it was said that some billionaire had bought his own island and brought the good doctor in to do some lab work. Time had gone by and it leaked out that they were trying to clone humans. The doctor's name was linked with the billionaire's but there had never been any charges brought up because of lack of proof and the island not being under any country's flag, being privately owned. Sheri looked up, Dick was across the room, reading paper work. She went over to him instead of calling him over, to show him what she had found.

"Dick I think I might have found a different angle." He looked up lost in his own thoughts and finally registered on her.

"Sorry I was just thinking, did you say something?" He asked.

"I think I might have found a different way we could look at things, I was looking into our scientist that was down at that makeshift lab in Georgia. Did you know that he was involved in cloning at some point? I was thinking, do you think that is why he was chosen to work with the soldiers? Maybe it isn't just the drug that they are testing, maybe they are testing it to see if they could put it into the DNA structure when cloning a human." Dick was silent, processing what Sheri had just said; he jumped up and started pacing.

"This is worse that I thought, I wondered about the drugs. Sure it made Quinn and Julie stronger and faster, magnifying their sensory abilities. But if this could be put into the genes, it could be intensified, more by cloning. You could make an army out of human clones and have them to fight wars for you. They would be better than humans, trained just to fight. This is really bad!!"

I joined him pacing, this was crazy; I couldn't believe that these kinds of things could be done. It reminded me of the movie Star Wars that I had watched as a child. Was this really possible in today's world? Is that why stem cell harvesting was such a big deal? Could they clone from the tissue? Is that why groups were always trying to block the research that could help save lives? Were they thinking life could be made better, created? Yes, I think anything was possible with the scientific advancement these days.

"We have to find that scientist! What about the lab in Georgia?" Sheri asked.

"That is the report that I was just reading. After Quinn told us his story, I sent a team down to find the place he was talking about and to retrieve Julie's friend, that had passed, Matt Turner. Quinn had the longitude and latitude so it wasn't hard to find, Matt and the lab. The place was empty, what a hell hole, they sent pictures back in the report, here take a look." Sheri looked at the dark hall with the dirt walls and the rooms that were worn down, falling apart. She felt respect for Julie to come out of there and not even complain. Maybe I was a little more girly than I thought, I don't know if I could have made it out of there unscarred like she did, Sheri thought to herself.

"Both Quinn and Julie are stronger than I thought making it out of a place like that alive," Sheri said, looking down at the blood stained floor in one of the photos.

"I expect it out of Quinn, he is a survivor, but little Julie is the one that broke him out." He said admiration in his voice. That was the kind of respect that Sheri was looking for she had a lot to learn from her new friend Julie.

"No wonder Quinn is taken with her," Sheri said.

"I think you are right and he doesn't even know it yet! Dick laughed, "I think you are a real asset working with us, a fresh view; no one else came up with what you just found and that is what they are paid to do. Great job!" Dick said, looking at her with respect. Sheri beamed, Dick had a way of making you feel good about yourself, no wonder people worked so hard for him.

The day passed fast, he called in the first three people putting them to work, finding the doctor. We had done everything that could be done for the day.

"Sheri did you want to go out to eat tonight or home to eat with my family?" Dick asked laying the papers he had been studying on the desk and picking up his jacket.

"If you don't mind can we go out? I haven't been to Washington to many times and wouldn't mind seeing some of the city while I'm here," she said.

"I know a great place to show you, it has really good steak and seafood and the best is the red wine. Some of the bottles are older that we are and the good years. It would be fun to try some of them. What do you think?" Dick asked.

"Sounds perfect! Just give me a moment." Sheri went into the bathroom and took off her suit jacket and straightened her black halter-top, un-tucking it and pulling it down over her black skirt. She looked in the mirror and took her hair out of its tight bun and let it tumble down her back. She liked what she saw; it was an easy transformation, for day to nightwear. Sheri stepped out of the bathroom rounded the corner and ran right into Dick.

"I'm ready," She said.

"Okay I am too, lets go out this way." He walked Sheri down the back halls to the elevator. Out of the corner of her eye she saw the guard in the elevator wink at Dick, as they left. Sheri liked it when Dick got embarrassed, his ears turned red, they seamed to be doing that a lot lately.

CHAPTER FOURTEEN

BRAZIL

The night was brisk as we moved in the darkness, the half moon guiding our way as we ran along the fence containing the marina. The salt-water smell of the ocean was carried in the breeze as I waited for the men to cut the fence open. We needed it big enough for Quinn to fit through, so we could get inside. They had been working on it for 10 minutes when everyone stopped as a harbor guard walked by making his rounds, down the dimly lit pier. A few seconds later we were inside and the fence put back in place. Walber whispered, not looking happy at being left behind.

"Quinn I need to go with you to make sure you are safe," he said, moving along the fence, trying to stop us from leaving without him.

"You have done enough for us, do not risk yourself anymore. I will call you soon, now here take this." Quinn handed him a roll of money and Walber handed it back. "Look you will take this and remember we are friends, what happened before couldn't be helped."

Walber nodded and took the rolled money, shoving it into his front pocket.

"Be safe my friend, until next time." I moved over and kissed him on the lips through the fence.

"Obrigado, my friend." Quinn and I moved into the shadows and we slowly walked along the wooded planks of the pier. Soft lights could be seen coming from the ship below the deck. Movement and muffled voices could be heard underneath the noise of waves hitting the side of the large boat. We moved around to the port side that was closest to the dock and Quinn put his ear against it to see what he could hear. He motioned me to follow him as we boarded the boat. Our bodies blended in with the darkness, we looked like ghosts as we moved around topside looking for a way to get into the belly of the ship. Layered in my bathing suit, then dive skins and the shorty dive suit, I felt a little warm but flexible in my tight cat suit looking outfit. Quinn had said it would keep us warm on our long trip. We had about an hour and a half to find a spot to hide that would be safe as we followed the drugs out of Brazil. Quinn found some small stairs off the stern of the boat that lead down into the dark under belly of the large ship.

As far as ships, this one was considered small. The beam was 50 to 80 feet, with the freeboard being what it should for a boat already loaded. There was a draft of at least 25 to 30 feet; it was hard to tell in the dark.

We moved into the bowels of the ship, passed the crew quarters, the kitchen and a few captains' cabins. Stairs lead farther into the ship to the area where the cargo was packed and the engine room. Voices could be heard clanging away on some of the pipes, preparing for the voyage. We traveled right, taking a turn away from the noise and found an area that we would have the least a chance of not running into anyone.

After moving some crates, a little fort was made in among the cargo, perfectly hidden.

"Julie I want you to go inside and take this." He handed me his backpack. "I will be right back." He was gone before I could react and

I was left just doing what I was told, not feeling happy at being left behind.

After a few minutes he returned carrying a case of bottled water and some extra food and crawled into our little hiding place. People were starting to move about on the topside, preparing the ship to leave, a lot of activity could be heard above. Quinn pulled out his international phone and made a quick call to Dick. I could hear the phone ringing and ringing before he picked it up.

"Dick is that you, Quinn here." He pushed the phone closer to his ear there was a lot of background noise.

"Hold on." Movement could be heard, as Dick must have been moving outside to be able to hear him better. "What is happening Quinn? Are you on board?"

"Yes all is a go, we will be pulling out in the next hour. Where you able to have the satellite turned to be able to track the ship," Quinn asked and I just looked at him and thought to myself that I might need to know the plan just in case something happened, I really did hate being left out.

"Yes, it's all set, be careful your phone most likely won't work once you are at sea," Dick said, "you two be careful."

"Understood sir, see you in a few days. By the way, how is it working out in Washington?" Quinn asked.

"Good so far, Sheri and I have found some new leads that we will fill you in on when you guys return. She is a lot smarter than I thought and found some things that none of my team was able to uncover. We are out getting a bite to eat as we speak, then we will head on back to my house. I better go if I stay out here to long she might get mad, I already saw some guys at the bar eyeing her and I can tell she doesn't want to be bothered." Dick said, trying to keep his voice down as he had walked back into the noise filled room.

"I will let you continue with that," Quinn said.

"Okay talk to you soon," Dick said.

"So how are Dick and Sheri getting along?" I said, smiling at the man of few words after he hung up the phone. He glanced over and gave my wet suit a tug and I fell on his lap.

"Not as good as we are but they are working together it sounds like they are finding out a lot. You are trapped with me for about three or four days, we will see what we can do to keep busy." He lowered his head to mine and gave me a soft kiss that sent the juices flowing right up my tight wet suit.

"I hope you brought the cards," I said, as I rubbed my palm over the stubble on his face. We settled in for the long boat ride.

The ship was underway within the hour. Noise could be heard from above as it moved through the water towards the open sea. The waves rocked the ship with steady motion I forced my eyes to stay open. But soon found myself sound asleep, safely in Quinn's strong arms. I was put into a false since of peace as we stowed away, forgetting the danger of the job that was ahead of us. Being with Quinn had made me feel that all was going to be okay. No one had come into our area of the ship and we settled down trying to stay quiet. The days passed slowly, I had taken off my wet suit, it was too warm and I put it on the floor to lie on. The air had turned warmer and my hair had curled up into blond locks that I tried to tie down. We felt the boat start to slow and Quinn started gathering our things tossing them into our backpacks

"What is it?" I whispered.

"The boat is slowing, come on, this might be where we are getting off."

"Get off! Oh shit, I didn't know we were going into the water!" I forced my wet suit back on and secured my things into my backpack. My heart was racing, but I was ready. Quinn was waiting, gun in hand, we moved out of our little hideout, towards the other end, of the boat. Under the stairs we waited in a dark corner. Men could be heard moving topside then heavy boots grew louder coming down the stairs, stomping hard on the floorboards, echoing off the walls as they rushed past us. We watched as they lifted a hatch in the belly of the boat. The hole was about six feet across. Down inside waves could be seen as the salty current licked the edges of the hole. About four men looked down into the water, before moving over to the crates. It was a long process as they put weights over the tops of each one, chaining them firmly in place and pushing the boxes over the edge into the dark water. When the job was finished, the hatch was put back down and sealed; the men went back up the stairs.

"Come on we don't have much time," Quinn motioned me to follow him back to the hatch and proceeded to open it back up. The sound of the engine was starting to get louder as it started to pick up it's pace. He handed me some goggles and a regulator that was hooked up to a small yellow canister. He put the canister inside my backpack and shoved the regulator in my mouth and started pushing me to the hole where the dark waters lay a few feet below. I could feel panic start to fill my body—oh no! He could have at least prepared me for this—are you kidding!

"Wait! " I whispered, taking the regulator out of my mouth. "You need to tell me what we are doing!" I whispered, tension in my voice. "I'm not a diver!"

"We don't have time! Hurry! Get in the water now! I will explain later. Please Julie go! Just breathe and I will be right there!" I jumped into the cool water, I felt a chill as it found it's way between my body and dive suit. I could hear the engine getting louder as my head went under the water, the noise intensifying as sound travels faster underwater. I breathed through my mouth, heart-racing, trying to calm myself. I felt tears the fall from my eyes, mixing with the salt water, snot filled under my nose inside my goggles, I floated under the ship. I was afraid that I was going to sink to the bottom and not be able to surface, that my tank would run out, it was so small. How much time did it give me underwater? Time seemed to go on forever, where was Quinn? I wasn't a diver, I wasn't afraid of the water but this was a little much, he could have told me to prepare my mind! Where is he? The engine was getting louder, water was moving faster around me, I felt a hand pulling me down and I started to struggle, I didn't want to go down any deeper. I felt a hand on my face, and opened my eyes and the darkness left showing rays of light as they filtered from the surface. It was Quinn motioning me to come with him; I started to move, taking his hand, following him down below the surface of the water. We swam hard and now I understood we had to get away from the boat or we would be run down. Soon the noise reduced, the waters movement slowed around us, we were alone floating under the water out in the middle of the ocean. I watched as small bright colored fish swam by, an orange fish that looked like a big gold fish about a foot long, swam up and I put out my finger, and it came to check it out. I was surprised that it wasn't afraid. Quinn tugged me to the surfaced and I felt I had a lot to say, now that we were alive.

"Why was I not informed of our plans? That was crazy, I could have died! What if I had freaked out?" I was hyped up and a little mad.

"Look Julie, calm down, I didn't know the plan until it happened. I just had the gear just in case," Quinn said, with that old grin on his face, he was enjoying this.

"From now on you need to keep me informed, if it has to do with me doing dangerous things that I am not sure if I can do!" I yelled.

"You did just fine," Quinn said smiling. "I knew you could do it."

"Well I just need to have a moment to wrap my mind around things, to prepare to do things I have never done before! You know I was tripping out! I think I had a panic attack, feel my heart it is still racing!"

"Look I wouldn't have made you do anything that I thought you couldn't do. You have a lot more in you than you think. Now come here and stop being mad. We have things to do." I floated over to him and grabbed his hand and he pulled me in closer.

"Alright Mr. Organized Bond, what is next?"

"I want you to stay right here while I go down and put a tracker on a few of the crates," he said.

"How long will it take? I don't want to drift away and be out here alone."

"Just a few minutes, don't move," he said, and started to lower himself in the water. I floated on the top of the water thinking about the man below the surface. He was dangerous in many ways, but a good man. I wondered what would become of us when this job was over; I sort of enjoyed the time and the excitement of being on the job with him. I had to hold on to my heart because he was a man that I was sure now could break it. I saw a flash in the distance and watched, wondering what it was, maybe a whale. I looked harder trying to see it again, as I floated on top of a small wave. Then it came to me, it was a boat; of course it was the boat coming to pick up the crates full of drugs, because it was getting bigger as I watched. Oh shit, where was Quinn? How much time had gone by? I put my goggles on and looked down into the water below. I could see Quinn working about 20 feet down. The man was going to be the death of me. I put my regulator in my mouth and dove under the water, swimming hard as I dropped down 15 feet and swam in his direction. He jumped when I touched his arm and looked me in the eyes as I tried to make him understand with hand movements that a boat was coming. He looked like he got it, quickly grabbing my hand we moved along the bottom. We swam about 50 feet kicking hard, getting as far away as possible. My body felt strong, but then I remembered the shots that we had been given. I wondered if it would last forever or would it wear off with time. When the distance was far enough away, we surfaced and tried to stay low in the water. The boat was now over the spot where the crates had been dumped and looked in the process of retrieving them. Divers had entered the water and a crane was pulling the boxes to the surface and stacking them on the deck of the small fishing boat. No one noticed us as we floated on the waves. We watched the boat pull away to the west until it was lost on the horizon. We could see a landmass in that direction, but it was hard to tell how far away it was.

"So do we swim?" I said, looking at him as he dug into his large backpack.

"Now, do you think I was going to make you swim for miles? By then we would be way off course in the drift of the current."

"Sorry Mr. Organized, James Bond, we are floating in the ocean." He laughed and pulled some blue rubber out of his bag.

"Now start blowing, you seem to have a lot of hot air." I looked at him and the wet plastic and started thinking curse words.

"Alright hand it to me!" I started to take it out of his hand and he produced a small gadget, which he hooked onto it and turned it on. The small boat started to fill with compressed air. "What else do you have in there?" He just smiled.

"It is a secret." It took about ten minutes as the rubber boat took shape. When it was full, Quinn lifted me out of the water and pushed me with his hands, cupping my ass as he lifted me into the boat. Once the backpacks where in the bottom, I pulled Quinn's large frame over the edge, his weight flattened one side of the inflated raft, letting water into the bottom. We lay there not moving for a moment, as the small boat rocked in the waves. Quinn produced a tiny motor hooking it to the back of the boat. What else did he have it there, it seemed never ending? He took out his phone and tried to call Dick but nothing happened when he dialed.

"Well it won't work out here just as Dick said, but I just wanted to try. Are you ready?" he asked.

"Ready for what? Are you going to tell my the plan?"

"No plan, just follow the drugs," he said, happy as could be, his golden eyes sparkling, his dark hair flowing around his shoulders. He really was enjoying the adventure and the risk taking, I could tell it made his blood flow. What a man! Yes he was all man.

We moved along in the direction the vessel had taken, the little craft went across the surface at a good pace. The day was sunny, in the 80's; my hair and suit had dried fast as the suns rays beamed down on us. The land mass got bigger as we approached, it looked to be a large island.

"Do you have any idea of where we are?" I asked.

"By my readings, I think we are approaching a small island in the north Caribbean. I'm not sure how close it is to the USA, but I know it can't be far."

We had traveled miles and the sun started to set. It was really beautiful, the island was getting closer and I could see the surf hitting the rocks along the shore. Quinn had picked up the pace. We needed to see as we approached and darkness was coming fast. We went around the island trying to find an easier place to get to the beach; this side of the island was covered in rock. The inhabitants of the island had to have a beach and it was most likely on the other side of the island, where the current didn't hit the island, so hard. Darkness came and we traveled around the west side where cliffs could be seen coming out of the water. They looked white with many eroded holes; looking closer I saw that thousands of white birds were covering the rocks, making their homes in the eroded surface. We rounded the curve of the face of the rock and were pushed in the direction of the rock face, the current was strong and we both paddled along with the small motor to stop us from crashing into the face of the rock. Are craft was pushed into a large cave, that the water had cut out over thousands of years. Quinn pulled inside the narrow passage, the entrance was about ten feet across and well hidden. It was dark and the moonlight didn't reach inside, I struggled to see as my eyes adjusted to the dark space. The passage narrowed as we continued forward until we were able to just squeeze through a small opening. The narrow channel widened after passage and we moved into a large pool of water cut into the stone.

"This is really cool!" I said, as I strained to see, waiting while my eyes adjusted to the darkness, of the small chamber. Quinn had stopped the engine and was digging in his backpack where he pulled out a flashlight. He put the light in front of us and moved it slowly around the room. We had found a place, that by the looks of it, no one had been for a long time. It was a round room that was as big as half a football field, the walls were smooth, polished by water over thousands of years, when the water level had been higher. We moved forward to a small sandy beach, it was covered in stacks of shells and discarded wood. Three old handmade wooden canons sat upside down in the sand, covered with old rotting pelts. We pulled onto the shore where the people of a different time had used this as a hiding place. It was exciting to be in a location that no one had been for so many years. I walked over to one of the canoes and saw some material coming out from under the space below. I gave it a tug, out came a rabbit skin and inside was polished rocks in the shapes of animals. What a find, someone had gone to a lot of trouble to do these, I put them back where I found them and went to see what Quinn was doing. He had moved to the outside of the beach area and was studying a small cutout step in the rock. I went over and watched as he flashed the light up the side of the smooth rock face to reveal steps that went up into the darkness above.

"I guess we are going up." I laughed, when he looked at me, I guess I was having a good time too. We went back down by the water and went through are backpacks to see what we were going to bring with us. Anything that we didn't need was left in the boat. I was happy to rid myself of the wet suit and the clothes underneath and put on my semi—dry clothes. I was surprised that they had stayed dry in the fancy old backpack. I felt much better out of the clothes that I had been in for the past few days and didn't think twice as I changed in front of Quinn. I watched and waited as he changed, trying to catch a glance of his nude bronze form in the dimly lit rock room, but he turned away reading the intent in my eyes. I looked in wonder at the scars that covered his back, now white in contrast to the golden shin.

"You're funny, I'm saving this for you for later!" He said.

"Ya right, you're just a tease," I said standing, "I can always feel my way," I took a step in Quinn's direction.

"Stay where you are, you don't want to start something that you don't want to finish." He stepped back away from my reach. When had I turned into, lusty women? He was driving me nuts!

"Who says," I said as I took a step closer. The laughter left his voice.

"Stop! Not now! We don't have time!

"Look what is wrong with you? I just want…Oh I don't know what I want." I stopped and just stood there feeling rejected. Was he not interested? His signals and body language said different. I had to put a wall up now or I was going to be really hurt. I backed away and was quiet, trying to swallow down the tears that I felt deep inside. I felt sick, how could have I allowed myself to care for him and he didn't feel the same. I must have been standing there for a while; I felt his hand on my check, pulling my face up until I looked into his eyes.

"The time will come, don't be upset with me. I can't be distracted, when the mission is over we will have time." He said his voice soft and tender, trying to make me understand what he was trying to say.

"What if the only time we have is right now, this moment? What if we don't come out of this alive or we are separated and there is never a time for us again."

"We will be okay, I will not let you get away from me, don't worry. Lets not talk about this anymore, come here." He pulled me tight against him and held me as he was proving that he would never let me go. He found my lips and kissed me with a force that ignited the blood, moving in my whole body. He kissed my hair, my eyes my face and reclaimed my mouth, I felt dizzy and pulled back from him.

"You are right, this needs to wait!" We both stood breathing hard, looking into each other's eyes, with a challenge.

"You have to understand that I want you, I just have to get the work done so that I can relax and we can really have the time to enjoy each other as we should." He moved from foot to foot waiting for me to say something.

"I understand, sorry, just a moment of weakness, I'm okay now." He put his hand out and took mine in his, we walked hand in hand to the small cut outs that were carved into the rock face, both of us working hard to focus our minds.

******

WASHINGTON DC

The past few days had gone by fast as Sheri worked with Dick on the case. Staying at Dick's house had been enjoyable. He had been the perfect gentleman. Everyday after work Dick had taken her out to different places to eat and small hide away bars in downtown DC. Sheri thought Dick was a really cool man and she felt that she could trust him as a good friend as she got to know him better every day. Sheri thought back over the time she had spent in the air force, it had been hard when it came to men, she had a few problems when she first started and from then on out had tried to avoid any relationships of any kind, with men. Sheri's weapon was that because of her looks she was always taken as one of those girls who looked good but had no brains and was treated as such. She had taken that negative and turned it into a positive using it against men, were she was able to use her body and looks to out smart most men and get what she wanted. So she was happy that with Dick for the first time he respected the intelligence of her mind and unlike most men he hadn't made one move on her, just put out his hand in friendship. He was the best boss that she had ever had and she wasn't about to do anything to mess their relationship up. Sheri like everyone that worked for Dick was engulfed in his great personality wanting to work hard to please him.

At the office, we had been working hard to find our scientist. He had just disappeared into thin-air; Sheri had a different angle to work on today. Instead of trying to trace him through a paper trail, she would try to find out, where the man might have worked over the years. She needed to find the island of his former employer and know the circumstance of their relationship. By mid-afternoon, Sheri had found the connection, the billionaire's wife had passed away and the husband had bought an island soon after and moved there years ago, no one had heard from him since. A thought entered her mind and she called Dick over.

"Dick, I think I know the connection between the scientist and the billionaire. I think it is stronger than anyone would think."

"Okay what have you got, run it by me." His full attention was on her and Sheri took a breath, wanting to get it right and slowed down.

"Well, I think that the scientist was brought to the island years ago by that billionaire for a purpose, not just for cloning or scientific research, but also for cloning the man's wife. The man had been with her for 26 years; she had been with him before he had made all his money and from what I read she would tell him the truth not what he wanted to hear. He was lost without her after she died and hears about the cloning of those sheep a few years back, it was a big story in the news. He searches for someone that knows or has done a lot of research in the cloning of animals with the idea of bringing his wife back. He tried different countries to see if he could do it there and gets turned down. As a last resort, he buys a private island and finds a doctor who he can also buy; the doctor is brought in, for a large amount of money agrees to give it a try. The doctor does his magic, the man gets what he wants and the doctor leaves the island. Years latter the doctor is again contacted, this time by our politician that wants him to take the cloning a step further, he agrees and starts injecting the soldiers in an attempt to take the blood from the soldiers that don't die. This is to be used in the DNA when the clones are made. This way, the clones are better than humans, disposable to be used where the government sees fit, because they really have no record of existing." Sheri took a breath, it sounded farfetched but for some reason it seemed to fit and she waited watching for Dick's reaction.

"That makes a lot of sense, but I bet that the government doesn't even know about any it. If they did, there would be no way this could have happened, too many people would have to know and this would have gotten out long ago. Someone inside would have leaked it to the press to stop it from going anywhere." Dick moved around and not thinking put his hand on Sheri's shoulder. She froze and then relaxed when she noticed that he didn't even realize that he had touched her.

"But that's not all, I think that if our little scientist did run into trouble or wanted to continue his research to make the perfect weapon, then I think he would run away to the billionaire's island. This way he could finish what he started and not be caught." I stepped out of his reach, acting like I was gathering up some papers and continued to talk.

"Do we know where that is?" Dick asked.

"Just found it, it is in the Northwest part of the Caribbean on the other side of Cuba." Just at that moment, one of his aides burst into the room.

"Sir, sorry to interrupt, we have had a beep show up on the radar, it is one of Quinn's trackers. We have been tracing the ship from the satellite, but it is not near where the tracker is beeping from." The man said, excitement in his voice.

"Where is the tracker coming from?" Dick asked.

"Sir, it is in the northwestern side of Cuba." Dick looked at Sheri and together they gathered the research papers and left the office.

"Call now and get a team ready, we leave within the next few hours!" Dick said. "We are going to an island." Sheri rushed after Dick following him out of the office, they had to go back to Dick's house to change their clothes.

Two hours later Dick and Sheri were flying south in a large army transport, with a team of about 12 marines, who sat against the sidewalls of the open cargo hold getting their weapons and gear ready for the drop. Being in the Air Force, Sheri had jumped in training many times, but none of them from the height that they were going to jump from. It was hard enough to hit the area on the ground but an island was a little harder, you had to be right on course or you could end up in the water.

The team had looked at Sheri funny when she had arrived with Dick, wondering who the girly girl was and why is she going with them? Looking at them Sheri hoped she could hold her own, at least she knew better than to show any fear, she hated proving herself to the men. Sheri looked over at Dick and he gave her a reassuring nod and went back to looking in charge bent over papers, making sure about the coordinates. They had been in the air for about four hours when the announcement was made to get ready. The flight had taken longer, because America had a no fly zone over Cuba. Everyone came alive, double checking their gear, talking among themselves, excitement in the air. The count down came "ten minutes," it was time to make our jump. Dick moved down to sit by Sheri and took her arm.

"I want you to stay with me in the air, we will go together. Okay?" Sheri nodded trying to look in control of her emotions in front of the men on the team. Inside, I was a little stressed and was acting real hard like this was a every day jump for her, but she was a little worried. The time was about up and Dick stood, they would be the first to go. He pulled a tag on my vest that turned on a small light also turning on a tracker in case she got lost. They moved to the door, a great rush of air hit them, as it was pulled back. Dick and Sheri stepped forward, he grabbed her vest and both took a step into the darkness.

The rush of air hit them and they were flying, soaring down to the earth. Watching her gage, the time came to pull my shoot, Sheri looked at Dick, and he nodded understanding, she pulled and was ripped out of his grasp. As Sheri looked around she could see the others in my group, their lights illuminated like fireflies floating in the breeze, they followed each other to the dark island below. As everyone came in closer to the earth, the outline of the island could be seen rising out of the sinister looking water. The surf could be heard as it broke over the jagged rocks below. Please let me land in a good spot was all Sheri could think; She didn't want to break anything or get lost in the ocean below. She watched the other's men's lights and followed them towards the top of a cliff. Sheri pulled right directing her shoot to the top of the rise and dropped to the top of the cliff, stumbling as she landed on her rear. Sheri sat for a moment checking herself to see if she was alright and then looked to see if Dick had made it okay. She let out a breath of relief when she saw him coming towards her with a smile on his face.

"You alright?" He shouted above the roar of the surf in her direction.

"Yes just fine," Sheri said, She struggled out of her harness, brushing the dirt and dried leaves from her clothes.

"You did really good!" Dick praised, "I was going to pull your cord for you and then you just did it right on time like a pro." He leaned down and untangled some of the lose cords from around her feet.

"Thanks Dick, I could have got that," watching him on his knees at her feet.

"Come on, lets gather the guys, we are going to have quite a hike before the sun comes up." They moved farther inland away from the edge of the cliff and started to locate all of the men.

CHAPTER FIFTEEN

We moved up the smooth surface of the rock face. Quinn had tied a rope around my waist, thinking if I lost my footing he would haul me up. But it turned out the other way around, the cut outs in the rock were small and his feet hardly grabbed hold. The people of the past had been a smaller than the ones of today. After watching Quinn struggling to climb up the rock face, I took the lead and found that it wasn't as hard for me. I would go up as far as the rope reached pull as he worked his way up the face of the rock. We came to a ledge, that allowed enough room for us to both stand with are backs to the rock face, catching our breaths. The steps had disappeared; behind us a dug out cave was molded in the earth, getting to my knees I searched moving towards the back looking for a hidden opening. The steps had lead to this location and couldn't just end, there had to be something, I searched in the dark and felt Quinn at my side handing me the flashlight. Behind a large boulder, we went through a gap and found a large cave that went inside the mountain. We moved inside following were it lead, after about a hour of moving uphill in the barely lit tunnel, we came to a dead end, the smell of fresh air loaded with the salt of the ocean overwhelmed us. We looked for an exit, it looked like a dead end, and Quinn and I were surrounded by dark earth, murky gloom enclosed around us, but hope was not lost.

"Can I see that for a moment?" I asked, taking the flashlight out of Quinn's hand, I slowly moved the light up and down the walls. There had to be a way out, I smelled it. On top of the dead end wall, way up top was a ledge and on the floor by our feet was old broken vines.

"They must have used the vines to climb up the wall, what are we going to do? It looks to be a good fifteen feet up." We were quite in thought trying to think of a way out, when an idea came to me. "Quinn do you think you could lift me on your shoulders? Then when I am there I will step on your hands and you could press me up. If I still can't reach, you will have to put your hands back down, then pump them up really fast and toss me in the air.

It is like a double stunt in cheerleading."

"I can do that, I know what you mean, I have never done it but I've seen it from the side lines when I used to play football," he said.

"You played football, I should have known. Was your name "the Viking?"

"Very funny, if you have to know, my nickname was "Killer" because I would kill the player, across from me. Now quit playing, come on, lets see if you still got it!"

"I still have it, it wasn't that long ago!" I retied the rope around my waist and climbed up the front of Quinn's body. He lifted me to his shoulders and we faced the wall. I judged I was about five feet away from the ledge, when my hands were positioned over my head, I was ready.

"Okay, take my feet in your hands, ready one, two, three—lift." Quinn pressed me with ease over his head and held me as I reached out and felt my fingertips grasp the edge. I stretched my body, trying to get a little higher in the air. Quinn went on his tiptoes and gave me about five more inches. Without telling me, he pumped his arms and tossed me in the air and I caught the ledge under my armpits. I used my upper body to pull my weight up and lay at the top breathing hard.

"What are you doing up there?" Quinn asked from below.

"I am trying to slow down my heart. Can you toss me the flashlight?"

"Here it comes." I reached over just in time to catch the beam of light. I turned and looked at the landing, it was large and at the end of the passage, I could see the moonlight through some branches. I tied the rope around a large boulder and tossed it over the side to Quinn below. Within a few moments, Quinn was by my side.

"That was fun!" I looked at him to see if he was for real, because I sort of felt the same way. I liked the excitement of this adventure with him at my side. I knew that with us together, everything would be okay, we were a good team.

"Come on, lets get out of here." We moved to the opening, no one had been in here for a very long time-the entrance was completely overgrown. It took us a while to work our way through the bushes, are hands and arms were scratched when we finished. Outside the air was fresh and we lay in the tall grass looking at the stars above as we recovered, taking in the beauty, breathing in the freedom of our escape from underground.

Quinn took out a gadget and a small beep, homed in on the crates we were following. It looked like they were still on the island; we got up and moved in that direction. The area we were in was overgrown and the entrance well hidden when we left, we didn't know if we might need to use it in the near future. We were on top of the cliffs and made out way following the edge so we wouldn't get lost as we as we made our way to the other side of the island. After a few hours we were looking down on a small harbor with a sandy beach, a house had been built, into the rock face. The home had large glass windows that looked out at the little harbor; light was reflected off the blue water sparkling a refection in the polished glass. No boats or guards could be seen, the place looked deserted from where we were positioned on the cliffs. On the edge, looking down, we found a small path, it looked like it hadn't been used in a long time, there was no foot-prints, just the little feet of small animals that lived up high among the brush.

"Are the drugs down there? What is that thing saying?" I asked, pointing to the device in Quinn's hand.

"It says that the crates are down below. I don't think it is as deserted as it looks. Come on, we need to see what they are doing with them." We moved forward down the trail. The sun had come up and the temperature had started to rise. I could feel the sweat run down my back under my backpack. Twenty minutes later and we were on the ground moving along the rocky shoreline. The ground was uneven, it slowed us down, finally we approached an out building on the edge, of the encampment. We studied the place and found there was just one door that leads into the place from the water's edge.

"Well that looks like the only way in. Do you want to wait here?" Quinn asked. I could tell he wanted me to say yes but it wasn't going to happen.

"Are you losing your mind? I'm not saying here alone! Anyhow, with your luck you're going to need me!"

"Ha, very funny, alright, let's leave our things out here so we can move more freely." I nodded and followed him into the trees where we hid our backpacks. With guns in our hands, we went forward in the direction of the door. I had brought my lock picking kit in my fanny pack around my waist; I got on my knees, to take a look at the door. Quinn turned the knob slowly pushing the door open.

"Don't forget, you have to always try it first Jr. Detective," Quinn whispered, smiling. He just loved to mess with me even when we were in danger.

"You just got lucky!" I said as I stepped in front of him and entered a hallway, it was a long room and the light was diffused, a door was at the other end and an elevator door was in the middle of the hall. We didn't see anyone around, slowly we moved down the hall to the door. This time we didn't get so lucky, the door was locked, it took me a few minutes to get it open; Quinn watched my back as I worked. We looked into the dark room as the heavy door creaked open. Against the wall were the crates stacked neatly. To the left side of the room was a large lab, stainless steel reflected in the light off my flashlight as I surveyed the room. At the back was a wooden door; Quinn and I moved to take a look. My heart was racing every step I took; it became louder in my ears. My gun, was in one hand, flashlight in the other, I crossed in front of Quinn in a police stance as I went forward to through the door. This one opened with the first turn of the wrist, after a few seconds with the pick, the heavy door moved out of the way. Inside I shined the light around and almost gagged at the sight that I was met with. Large round glass containers came from the floor housing what looked like babies in the womb. They were all about the same age, judging from their size, they were all about six months—old. Umbilical cords attached to machines, working as if inside a mother's body.

"What is going on here? I thought they were making soldiers better, I didn't know they were making them from scratch!" I was freaking out at the possibilities of what had been done to these babies floating in front of me.

"There is way more to this then we even thought. Lets go up, we need to find landline and call Dick. This isn't in our hands any more; we need to call in the forces to take care of these babies," he said, watching the machines as the monitors beeped.

"You don't think they will kill these children because of what has been done to them? Do you?" I asked. I didn't want any harm done to the innocent, that couldn't protect themselves.

"I'm not sure, this isn't for us to decide," Quinn said and I agreed and moved to follow him, shutting the door slowly and looking back at the dozen small children, wondering if this was the future of civilization.

We relocked the main door and entered the elevator. There was only one button, we pushed it and it started to rise. The doors opened into a large living room full of people. I looked around the room and felt tense as a man stepped in front of us. I recognized him but for a moment didn't remember where I had seen him before.

"Well Quinn, it has been a long time. What took you so long?" Quinn stepped in front of me blocking me from the man, I could hardly see around him to look at the thin man holding a gun. "I thought you would have been here sooner, losing your touch?"

"Just taking a tour of the lab downstairs," Quinn said, I watched as the man stiffened.

"Well that's unfortunate that you had to see that. I was thinking we could some how make a truce between us and work together. But I know you, after seeing what is downstairs there is no way you could be convinced now."

"Steve Smith, there was never a chance that I would ever turn against our government for personal gain." The thin, brown-haired man moved the gun he was holding and positioned it close to Quinn's head.

"That's too bad, I did like you at one time." Everything happened so fast, I heard a voice yell out and saw her dive at Smith, a wild dark haired woman flashed across my line of vision. She came out of nowhere, flinging her body into his and knocking him to the ground. The gun went off and I watched the women fall to the floor dead at our feet. Smith was up again, focusing on Quinn, positioning the gun once again, not affected by the dead women at his feet. Quinn stood not moving as if in a trance. He had fallen to his knees and was rocking the body of Nicole in his arms. I raced around him; my gun had been knocked out of my hand in the commotion. I pulled the only weapon I had on me from the inside of my bra and rushed the man. Mace went into his eyes and he pulled the trigger as he fell to the floor the bullet hitting Quinn on the side of the head. He dropped to the ground and all I saw was blood. My eyes swam as I jumped on Smith's back; he struggled to gain control of the gun. I reached under my shirt and pulled out the syringe that I had carried all these weeks and stabbed him in the eye with it, pushing the stopper down letting the drug flow, into his blood stream. He screamed in pain.

"I am going to kill you! You fucking Bitch!" He moved getting ready to jump me as I pushed myself against the wall. I closed my eyes, waiting for the sound of gunfire and heard a groan, Smith fell to the floor. I slowly got to my feet moving to Quinn's side, tears flowing down my face. My heart ached at the thought of losing him. I kissed his check the blood was still forming a puddle under his head. I touched his neck and fell backward on to the floor.

"He's alive, oh shit! What do I do? Get yourself together, he's alive." Move! I told myself, you're talking to your self! I took off my shirt and folded it and tied the long sleeves together around his head. I went to the back of the living room where three other people were sitting down on the floor hiding out. They looked non—threatening so I left them alone and moved to the kitchen. I came back to Quinn with a Tupperware bowl full of water and a clean washcloth. I moved back through the living room, I yelled for someone to find me a needle and some thread. Without looking, I moved to Quinn's side and found the shirt, red soaked with his blood. Soon a young girl by my side with the requested needle and thread, she didn't make a move to leave and sat watching as I removed the shirt from his head and proceeded to clean and stitch him up. The wound still seeped blood but the shirt had stopped the flow.

"Do you have anything to kill the germs?" I asked and the girl disappeared and returned with some Neosporin. "Thanks," I said, as I applied a large amount to the wound and covered it with the clean rags and taped it to his head. That was the best I could do, the job was done. I sat back and looked at my work, well it wasn't the best, but blood wasn't leaking through the cloth now. I looked at the girl for the first time, she was a pretty thing with long white blond hair; her hair matched her delicate white skin; she had the face of an angel. Her lips curved in a soft line as her frail hand settled on my arm.

"I'm Julie," I said, trying to make my voice calm.

"Ester" she said so soft I almost didn't hear, she was young, I took her to be about thirteen. After checking to see if Quinn was breathing okay, I moved over to the girl that had got herself killed trying to save him. I knew it was Nicole; she had a soft look now that she was dead. The bullet had hit her between the eyes; there had been no pain, just instant death. I slowly moved over to Smith's side. His face was red where I had sprayed him and his eye puffy and closed where the Needle had gone into his eye. He was out cold but I could see his chest rise and fall, he was alive. I turned to my new friend, "Could you get me some rope?"

She moved without saying a word and was back at my side in a few seconds, she wanted him tied up fast, her hands were shaking and she looked scared as she watched Smith. I flipped him on his stomach and proceeded to hog tie the bastard. When I was done, I checked Quinn again and moved into the living room to see if the two men on the floor were all right. One was old with a balding head, the other I recognized,

"Doctor Belvar?" I asked as I moved toward the cowering men. The doctor's head came up and I saw that he recognized me too.

"What is going on here and why were you giving soldiers the shots in Georgia?" I asked, my voice going hard remembering all the men that had died along with my friend Matt.

"I was following orders just like you were. When the American government found out about what we did with Ester, we were forced into developing a weapon for the US Government," Belvar said, looking like a weak man as he huddled in the corner.

"Whom in the government are you talking about? From what I understand the President doesn't even know this is happening! Who is in charge?" I yelled, I was about to lose it; my adrenalin was pumping hard through my body. "What have you done to Ester?" I said, looking at her, protection rising in me.

"You don't understand the importance of all this do you? Ester is a clone of his wife," he said, looking at the older man who was just sitting looking out the window. "We made Ester to replace her but at the time he didn't understand that she would start life as a baby, not a full—grown human." I looked at the old man; he turned his head away before saying anything.

"I have waited thirteen years for Ester to grow up, on her 16th birthday she will become my wife in all ways." I looked at Ester, she was backing up slowly and putting her body behind mine, a pleading look in her eyes.

"Sir, I think she looks at you like a father, not a lover," I said, pushing her behind me.

"I made her for this purpose! She will be my wife!" He yelled, his face turning red on his pink skin. He must have been totally out of his mind or in a fantasy. I felt Ester behind me shaking and understood that they wouldn't let me leave this island alive; the cloning was too much of a secret. I watched as the old man pulled out a small gun that had been sitting in the palm of his hand and aimed it at me. GREAT! Keep them talking, this gun shit was starting to make me mad.

"What about the babies downstairs, what will happen to them?" I asked the men looked at each other.

"Well we are happy you showed up, we have been trying to find the two of you."

He made a swiping jester towards Quinn. "You two are the only ones that made it through the series of shots, we need your blood to make the babies complete. They will be born as weapons for the government and we will be paid a very high price for them," the old man stated.

"Why is it always about money with you people?" I backed slowly to toward the elevator, watching them both as I backed up.

"Stop or I will shoot!" The old man said, he pointed his gun at my chest.

"No Father!" Ester stepped in front of me blocking his shot. "No more killing! Kill me instead!" She stood in front of me not backing down as; I pulled Quinn into the elevator.

"We can work this out Ester, I love you!" He stood up, his legs shaking as he took aim. I grabbed her hand and yanked her into the elevator just before the door closed behind us. We heard a shot ring in the air, behind us as we descended to the main floor.

"Is this the only way in and out of there?" I asked as motioning upstairs, the doors opened.

"Yes," she said looking sad.

"Don't worry, it will all be okay. You didn't want to marry him did you? If you want to stay, I won't try to stop you." She looked at me, wisdom in her eyes beyond her years and shook her head.

"No, lets go!" she whispered in her quiet voice. We moved out of the elevator and I dragged Quinn behind us, not able to move to fast with his weight more than doubling mine. I put a crate blocking the door so it wouldn't close making the elevator remain on the lower level. They would be trapped up stairs until someone came and let them out.

I was trying to put Quinn on my shoulders when I heard movement down the hall.

"Get behind me," I ordered. Ester jumped behind a crate where I had laid Quinn and I kneeled as men in dark suits rounded the corner, guns drawn.

"Hands up! Drop the piece!" One of them yelled. I dropped my gun, there was too many of them, I put my hands in the air. I heard a voice that I recognized, and was relieved, it was Dick.

"Dick! It is me, Julie, I yelled down the hall. He stepped to the front motioning the men behind him and they fell in against the wall of the long hall.

"Julie! Are you guys okay? We tracked Quinn's tracker on the crates here to the island."

"Quinn is hurt, we need to get him some help! This is my friend Ester, we have to get her out of here!" I yelled down the hall coming out where Dick could see me, pulling Ester behind me.

"Sheri!" Dick Yelled, Sheri came from outside at a jog and stood moving next to Dick, concern on her face when she saw the shape Quinn and I were in. "Take four men with you back up to the top, have them carry Quinn and Julie's friend Ester. Call in the transport to land up top, we will be there shortly." I watched Sheri nod and returned with four men, Ester looked nervous about leaving my side her eyes were pleading with me not to leave her.

"Go on, I won't let them kill him. It will be okay; you are safe with Sheri, she is my friend." Sheri moved over and took her hand; Ester looked at the model-like woman and went with her. It was easy to get people to trust you when you looked like Sheri.

"Now what has been happening here?" I briefly filled him in on what had occurred and Smith, the doctor and the owner of the island that were upstairs. He decided to leave the men where they were for now and send back a team to retrieve them later. We had to leave to get Quinn some help and the President had to be called and filled in on what had been happening.

"Sir, Dick, I have to show you something, this isn't all of it. Wait until the President hears about what I am about to show you. Come with me."

"Men you stay here and guard the area." We moved down the hall, to the door at the end of the hall through the crates to the wooden door.

"This is a little shocking," I said, I turned on the light. One of the babies opened her eyes. I jumped, feeling a little shocked. Dick stood motionless, staring at the glass tanks, taking it all in.

"We will have to move fast on this one. They are cloned...Right?" Dick asked.

"Yes, they were going to insert Quinn and my DNA into their bodies to make them real weapons. What a plan," I said, thinking of little

Quinn's running around smashing things like Bam Bam from the Flintstones.

"They will move them to the US. Who knows what will happen," Dick said.

"I know they will need that doctor Belvar upstairs to monitor them until they are born. He has been successful in the past," I said.

"How do you know? I have never heard of any human clones...I will make sure he goes wherever the babies do. By the way, what is up with your little friend?" Dick asked.

"What? Ester?" I didn't want to say it. "She is...a clone of the man's wife, the one that owns this island. Can we not tell the government? They would make her live at a lab; she could live a normal life if she lived with me. Well, semi-normal." Dick stood in thought.

"You're kidding! I can't believe that it is really possible! Okay I think you are right, but it could never get out! Never! But instead why don't we have her live at my family's home. We have plenty of space. My mom would love having my long lost child of an old romance show up in my life. She thinks I need to fill the home with kids anyhow. What do you think? You could always come stay for how ever long you want to."

"You're a really good man Dick." I said patting his arm, I felt better now that that was solved.

"What are you talking about?

"That I think you have a good heart."

"Now don't be getting a crush on me Julie, Quinn would get mad."

"Hay, I can't help it if he isn't interested. Anyhow, when the girl upstairs lay dead in his arms, he froze and that almost got him killed. He was really hung up on her and that doesn't help my cause." I felt sad because I had said the truth and by saying it out loud, it made it sink in. He wasn't going to be ready for a relationship anytime soon.

"You have a lot to learn little girl," Dick said as he put his strong arm around me and kissed the top of my head. "You are going to be alright, you're a strong one. Quinn will come around, everyone sees your connection but the two of you."

"Sometimes you don't want to be the strong one, he can really hurt me Dick."

"I know," he said. We walked out of the room shutting the door tight, the men followed us to the top of the bluff where an army chopper was waiting to take us back to Washington.

******

WASHINGTON DC

Forty-eight hours later our small group had set up our headquarters at Dick's family's estate. Upon arriving we were greeted at the door by Ann with open arms looking past us she saw Ester standing by the car door. We had explained to her that she would have a new family and would be Dick's daughter, at first sadness had filled her eyes and was soon washed away as she saw the possibility's of a different outcome for her life. She stepped into Ann's embrace and smiled at the small girl who took her hand.

"I'm Amanda," the blond little girl said jumping up and down. "Daddy said you were going to be my sister!" Excitement filled her voice as she showed off hopping on one foot and smiling at the taller thin girl.

"I'm Ester and I'm sure we are going to be good friends." She was pulled away from Ann, Amanda taking her hand and leading her up the front steps, tugging her along, using all her small weight as the frail girl was pulled behind her.

"Come on Ester, I want to show you to your new room, I helped get it ready for you. I like pink but daddy thought you would like a pale yellow to match your hair. Ester looked back at Dick and gave him a quick grin before letting Amanda pull her away.

"He was right, I do like yellow," she was tugged to the door. Ester looked over her shoulder and asked Dick, "is it okay if I go with her?"

"Go ahead, don't let her wear you out, we will all see you at dinner," Dick turned to say something to his mother but she had already followed the girls into the house.

"Bring a child home and I get no attention!" We followed Dick, Quinn and I were taken to Dick's wing of the house and shown into a large bedroom done in light blues. In the middle of the room sat a large bed that had a step to get on top because it was so high off the floor.

"I thought you two could share since you would sleep in the same room any way," Dick said as he helped Quinn with our backpacks. Quinn still seemed a little weak from getting knocked out after being shot in the head. The bullet had hit him in the temple, grazing through some hair as it knocked him out.

The doctor had said that he had been out longer because of lack of blood, but that if I hadn't sewed him up, he would have had a hard time recovering. He was to rest for a few days and would be as good as new. He was trying to act like he was fine but I could tell that he was tired.

"Quinn, why don't you rest and I will wake you when it is time for dinner," I said.

"What are you going to be doing?" He asked.

"I am going to go with Sheri and borrow some clothes until I can get to the store, then I will find something for you in Dick's closet," I said moving to the door with Dick and Sheri.

"Alright, what is mom cooking for dinner? I am going to be really hungry!" Quinn said, as he moved in the direction of the bathroom as we left the room.

"Whatever it is, she will have a lot of it my friend, now rest!" Dick said as we moved to the hall leaving Quinn alone.

"Do you think he is going to be okay?" I asked watching Dick's reaction.

"He will be just fine, I have seen it before, he's just needs to rest he is stronger than you think. It is more his ego, than his damaged than his head. You saved his life, he froze when the girl was killed, he feels the necessity to protect you not be saved by you."

"That is a bunch of BS! We are a team; I'm not a weak woman that needs protecting. We are equals and men new to understand that I can take care of myself!" I said, trying not to yell in the hall so that Quinn would hear me outside his door talking about him.

"Don't get mad, I'm just saying it might work better to your advantage if you played the weak women role for a night." I thought about what he was saying, Quinn had been pretty distant for the past two days. I had thought he was just feeling bad but now I understood what Dick was saying.

"He's right," Sheri said, softly putting her hand on my arm and pulling me in the direction of her bedroom. "Dick, we will see you tonight at dinner." Looking over her shoulder she smiled at him with a look to let him know that she would take care of it. After the door to her bedroom was closed she burst out, "I don't know what I am going to do?" I turned and looked at her not knowing what she was talking about.

"What is wrong?" I asked as I watched the pretty women unclip her hair and move to sit on the window seat looking over the flower garden.

I sat on the bench beside her and looked at the beautiful view—the bright flowers in stark contrast to the green grass was a sight, but they were no comparison to the lady sitting waiting for my attention. She really was lovely, the women I had befriended. "What is going on, why are you upset?"

"I have been here for the past few weeks and have never had such a dilemma. Dick has informed me that he might put in a request that I come and work for him with the CIA and I needed a second opinion."

"Well that's great what is the problem?"

"I just need to make real sure that it is for my skills at my job that I am wanted. I have had trouble in the past and made some bad decisions changing offices in the air force moving up and found that it was because the boss wanted me close not just for my skills but because they wanted to have sex with me."

"To be honest I think that Dick isn't like that, he is kind of a straight arrow. Has he done anything to lead you into thinking other wise?"

"Not at all, I feel much better now and I can be excited about the change, how exciting to work for the CIA!"

"Your not kidding, maybe you could put in a good word for me."

"Now what are you going to do about Quinn?" Sheri asked? "He seams to be in a real funk like Dick implied."

"I don't know what to do he has been acting funny for the past few days, I just thought he was still trying to get over the girl."

"Well who knows what goes around in the minds of some men, but to start out tonight we can start by you looking very female at dinner. With no threats, it will be like going on a date in the house. Then you and Quinn can go to bed early together and everything will be fine between you two tomorrow.

"Good thinking, the only problem is that Quinn and I haven't slept together and that could add to the stress between us. Well we have slept together in the same bed but not slept together in the biblical since." A shocked look crossed her face that I saw her quickly cover up.

"I just thought that the two of you, well the way you act together, it had looked to me that you were a couple." I put my head down. Was this so obvious to others and not to me?

"He wants to wait, until when I'm not sure, but it is driving me crazy. I have never had to chase anyone and he has turned me down so many times that I have given up and decided that he has to be the one to make the move, when he thinks the time was right."

"What is his reasoning behind that? Sheri asked.

"He thinks that his job puts having a relationship on the back burner because of the danger. To be honest, I think he isn't over the women that he was sleeping with in Brazil, remember the evil one that was upstairs. But maybe she wasn't so bad, she died saving his life."

"I see it clearly now. He is mentally fucked up and doesn't want anyone else he cares about getting killed. The problem is he is fooling himself because he already cares about you and if he thinks by just not sleeping with you he is going to save you from getting killed, he is crazy. It is too late for those thoughts, you have already taken his heart." I looked at her, she was so sure of herself.

"You're a romantic, I wouldn't go that far, but I know he would miss having me around, we make a good team," I laughed at the two of us; it was nice to have someone to talk to. In high school I was one of the girls that always had a boyfriend and it kept me from that close relationship with the girls. "Well aren't we a pair!" We fell into silence both thinking of our own dilemmas as we watched the sunset over the garden.

At dinner that night I could tell all was not well with Quinn, he would barely look at me and I wondered how I was going to pull sleeping in the same room with him and his wounded ego. I was starting to get a complex, Dick and Sheri held most of the conversation at the table. The focus was on the kids, I noticed the girls blooming friendship, Amanda was so taken with Ester she wanted her attention at all moments. Ester was patient, softly telling her to pay attention when her father was speaking to her. Amanda would do whatever she was asked to do by Ester, wanting to please her, so happy to have a sister. Soon the girls and Ann retired to their areas of the house and the four of us were left at the table. The conversation had turned to the island and what had happened there. Instead of giving a play by play of Quinn and my encounters, I steered the conversation to the babies downstairs.

"What happened to the babies and the doctor? Did you find out what was going to happen to them?" I asked as my voice trembled. Out of the corner of my eye, I caught Quinn look in my direction before quickly turning his head.

"What babies?" Sheri asked, looking my way.

"The doctor was cloning babies," I said, turning my head to Dick "What happened to them?"

"The government decided to leave them where they where and not chance trying to move them. The doctor is staying as well until they are born, along with about thirty marines to guard them."

"What happened to the owner of the island?" I asked.

"You didn't know?" He asked.

"What?"

"A team was sent back after we left and found that the old billionaire had shot himself in the head and was dead. The doctor was hiding in the corner and Smith was gone, a window had been broken and he had escaped down the front of the glass windows," Dick said, looking at Quinn.

"He always was resourceful, we were taught to survive," Quinn said looking down thoughtfully.

We heard the doorbell ring and Ann call out that she would go get it; the staff had left for the night. A few seconds later, Ester rushed in the room, pulling Amanda behind her and crawled under the white tablecloth. At first I thought the girls were just playing until I felt a tug on my pants and I looked into the eyes of the older frightened girl.

"What is it?" I whispered.

"Bad man," was all she said and ducked back under the table. Quinn had heard her and moved to the wall of the entryway and ducked behind the china cabinet. A moment latter Steve Smith pushed Ann into the room. He looked dirty, he had a over grown beard his clothes were wrinkled and torn, he carried a gun in his hand, his eyes looked wild, desperation came from his pores. I saw Dick tense across the table when he saw the frightened look on his mother's face.

"You thought this was all over didn't you?" Smith said looking at Dick. "You and your fancy house and your fancy family."

"What do you want?" Dick yelled "Let her go and get the hell out of here!"

"I want what you have taken from me!" Smith said gripping Ann around the throat, breathing hot breath on her neck, making her turn her head away from him as he gripped her hair. She tried not to move or struggle, knowing what the results would be.

"What is it, you feel, I have taken from you?" Dick's voice echoed in the large room, the forcefulness of it demanding command.

"I want you to get the Marines off of the island now, make a call and I will leave. The doctor and the babies are mine; they will go to the highest bidder! I have worked too hard this past year to make this happen." His eyes were wild staring at Dick. He gripped Ann tighter making her cry out.

"The island isn't even yours. How are you going to manage keeping it?"

"I had the old man sign it over to me before I helped him shoot himself." A gasp was heard from under the table and I felt a gun get pushed into my hand. I took it and watched as Quinn moved in silently behind Smith, who was preoccupied talking to Dick. Everything happened fast. Before I knew what was going on, Quinn had made his move, putting his arm around Smith's throat cutting off his air supply, Smith dropped his hands that had been holding Ann breaking the connection trying to remove Quinn's strong arms from his throat. He held still know Quinn held his life in his hands, knowing if the roles were reversed he would kill the large man. Ann was knocked away in the motion falling to the floor, her hair had came out of her bun and she looked older as she tried to steady herself. I jumped over the table knocking the chair to the floor with a big bang, when Quinn and Smith fell to the floor.

"Dick!!" He turned and caught the gun that I threw in his direction.

I dove landing on top of Ann blocking her from the men that were in a life and death struggle on the polished floor. I shoved her under the table and watched as Dick shot Smith in the shoulder and Quinn knocked him out. Sheri had leapt out of the way and now stood over the body with the napkin ties from the table in her hand. She pushed Quinn boldly out of the way and tied Smiths hands behind his back, proceeding to tie his feet. I had rushed to Quinn's side and embraced his big bulk in my arms, checking him for injuries.

"You're alright?

Aren't you?" I pulled at his clothes checking out his body, making sure he wasn't bleeding.

"I'm fine, are you okay?" He asked.

"You are so brave my big Viking!" I said, still holding him, not about to let him go, clinging to him as he tried to move out of Sheri's way.

"So are you, my little marine, now let me up," he said starting to struggle underneath me, pushing me to the side of him.

"I can't, I think I broke my hand, I landed on it wrong." He took it gently in his big hands and inspected it; his lips lightly touched the swollen area by my thumb.

"We'll get you some ice, I don't think it looks broken." He stood with me in his arms and left the dining room moving to the kitchen where he opened the freezer and pulled out a bag of frozen vegetables and laid them in my palm. He carried me back to the dining room where everyone was waiting for the military to come pick up Smith, who was still knocked out cold, a towel wrapped tightly around his shoulder to stop the blood from dirtying the floor.

"It's a shame about Smith, he was a good agent in the field," Dick said, addressing Quinn.

"I know, one time he saved my life, but that was long ago before greed and power became the force that drove him." Quinn looked sad.

"What happened to him?" I asked.

"He lost his wife and son to a friend. When he came home one time from being out of the country, he found them just gone. At times we could be gone for months with no correspondence to anyone in the states, it made it hard to have a family. His friend was a man who worked in the stock market and had lots of money. I think that made him think that money must be what was important and he turned into a different person. He didn't take into consideration that he was a violent man and his wife got tired of the fights and beatings from him." Quinn looked thoughtful as he spoke. Dick also looked sad. This kind of work that has a threat of death and violence could change a weak person into a loose cannon. The men in uniforms came soon after and took Smith away in a large dark van with blacked out tinted windows. He would be debriefed; military justice would decide what to do with him. He had been a great service to the government in the past. When he was gone the girls came out of hiding. I had forgotten that they were under the table.

"Are you girls all right?" Sheri asked as she gathered them up and walked them from the room.

"Ester," I called, the young girl turned. She, like her real father, was rich, everything would go to her, and Dick would make sure of it.

"Thanks," we smiled at each other with an understanding as she left the room. Ann stood straightening her clothes and smoothing her hair with dignity, acting as if this happened all the time. She was a strong women and I saw where Dick had gotten his strength from.

"I think that I will retire to my room if I am not needed." Ann turned and left, her head held high.

"Goodnight mother," Dick said to her back as the four of us followed looking back at the disarray left behind for in the morning.

"I think you can put me down now," I said as Quinn's arm tightened, he was carrying me like a baby and it was a little embarrassing. But it was better than the past two days, so I allowed him to do it, feeling the closeness to him that I liked when I was in his presence.

"I think I won't." He moved towards the stairs and turned to Dick. "The four of us need to meet in the morning after breakfast, how about in the sitting room?"

"Lets say around 10:00 am because it will be Saturday. I will have breakfast served upstairs in the sitting room as you call it." Quinn and Dick nodded and I was carried away before I could say goodnight to any one.

"Goodnight," I said as I was carried up the staircase and down the hall, to the blue bedroom and dumped in the middle of the fluffy comforter. My bag of vegetables fell to the floor as I lay back on the comfortable bed lost in the soft blue pillows. I looked up to find Quinn watching me.

"What are you doing? Come here." I ordered.

"Just thinking about what I am going to do with you." He looked intense, not this again. "I have been thinking the past few days on what to do about you. For all the walls that I put up, you seem to knock them down. I find myself not in control of the situation when you are around. It scares me." Wow I didn't know what to say so I just sat silent, I knew I had to say something, but I just wanted it to be the right thing.

"Quinn…your not the only one that is afraid to take a chance, but in life if you don't take that chance you will never know what could have been or what you missed. I'm scared too; I would rather have a moment of happiness than a life of ordinary. You have to decide what you want." It was silent in the room as he processed what I had said and slowly he answered me.

"I want you!" He said softly as he moved to the bed and took me in his embrace. I felt him shake as emotion passed between us.

"I want you too! There were no more words as we removed each other's clothes. Passion had over taken us both, we rolled around on the bed, both of us wanting to be on top and be in charge. At last Quinn lay back and looked at me, giving me free-rain of his body, he put his hands down to his sides and I watched as he clenched his fists. I licked the skin around his nipples, not touching the nipple. I kissed his checks and his face and his hair, but not touching his lips. His hand had gripped the bedding tightly, trying to stay still. I moved down his stomach, kissing and licking, biting his abs as I moved lower, following the light trail of hair as it went down in the direction of his groin. When I got to the waist band of his briefs Quinn shuttered and rolled on top of me pinning me and knocking the air out of me as he pressed his lips to mine and held me with his large body, taking charge. I just let him. Hours latter slumber overtook us both, morning coming sooner that either of us thought as we scrambled into the shower to prepare for the day, both of us with a smile on our faces as we went to breakfast.

CHAPTER SIXTEEN

I felt giddy as we quickly moved down the hall to the sitting room, happiness surrounded us, and we could both feel it. A strong connection had been made between us, not to say that we didn't have one before but it was almost like the sex had sealed the deal. The uncertainty and the pressure was gone, leaving just peacefulness that surrounded us. At the door I stopped, Quinn looked at me with a look of "What?" and I put my arms around him, softly kissing him as I felt him respond, I pulled away and ran my hand over my face and put on a calm one to replace the look of joy, Quinn laughed and we entered the room. Inside Dick and Sheri sat on the small sofa in front of the fire. They looked like they were in a heavy conversation. Both stopped talking when we came in the room, Quinn and I went to the couch and took our seats around the warmth of the stone fireplace.

"What's going on?" I asked looking at Sheri. She looked at Dick and back at me. Her expression told me that she wasn't happy about something.

"We have to finish with this case and Dick thinks I should be left here to watch the children!" She stomped her foot on the floor to show her anger.

"Now that isn't what I said!" He stood pacing the room, straightening papers on the desk, doing busy work other than fight with Sheri.

"In a round—about way, you did. You said you need someone to watch and make sure the children are safe. You know that is BS and I won't do it! I am well-trained and can take care of myself!" Sheri yelled rising to her feet, her jaw in a determined strong line. She was even pretty when she was mad.

"I just don't see any reason in making you go back to that place, you're to much of a lady!" Frustration was in his voice, it did sound a little lame on his part, a weird way to say you care and don't want her in danger.

"You are too strong of a man to put your wanting to protect my honor in front of the job, you're being silly, I am going! Remember I am the one who got the senator's fingerprints in the first place! I am the one who will recognize him and reel him in!"

"That was before you were under my protection!" Dick stammered.

"I am under no one's protection and can take care of myself! I am the one that the man will want, the one that got away. You need to relax, there's no changing my mind!" Sheri sat down and crossed her arms over her chest and looked at the fire. Dick moved over to the window and stared outside not saying anything else. Quinn and I looked at each other and I couldn't help but bust out laughing. Quinn started and I couldn't stop the giggles, the chuckle had me and I was gasping for breath as I held my side.

"You two need to get laid, you're both a little uptight!" I said holding back another round as Quinn thought it was funny and tickled me until I fell to the floor crying for mercy. Dick and Sheri forgot about being mad at the sight I must have made. I was on the floor covered with Quinn; he was trying to get me to say "Uncle."

"What's up with the two of you?" Dick said, through my tears I saw his face, he understood that Quinn and my relationship had taken a turn.

"Now I see what is happening, maybe we do need to get laid Sheri." The room was filled with laughter. "When you two are finished we can get down to business." We both straightened brushing the tears from our faces and took our chairs trying to hold back the giggles that I felt begin to raise to the surface again. Sheri uncrossed her arms and looked across the room at Dick with pleading in her eyes, asking for forgiveness.

"Sheri and I were talking about tonight as I am sure you picked up on. I just don't like using her for bait! But we do need to pick up the organizers of this operation. We have enough to send them down the river from the bugs and phone tapes that we had installed.

Tonight we will be wired, to get the senator on tape, he is the one giving the orders and somehow we need to make him admit it. Smith was mad when the senator didn't lend a hand in helping to get him released, so he has given evidence that proves the senator was deeply involved, pulling major strings to make it happen with some of his friends that owed him favors.

"I was telling him that I am the only one that can make this work because I have already been inside and had contact with him," Sheri stated sternly.

"I don't mean to go against you Dick but Sheri is right, she is the most important person to make this work," I said, he frowned and Sheri smiled at me. Anyhow, I am going to need her to help me through the night, we will go in together as girlfriends, out for a good time." Quinn now was making a face. "Get over it boys! We don't have time for your macho manly stuff, now we have to organize." The room stopped, everyone serious.

"Macho manly stuff, who has that?" Dick said looking at Quinn. "Okay lets get started."

The breakfast hour went into afternoon as plans were made, around 4:00 PM an early dinner was wheeled in and put on the table in the corner. We all ate the tasty food prepared by Dick's chef. Time had passed by and Sheri and I escaped into her room to get ready for the night. She pulled out a few outfits that could fit me and we went to trying them on, I fell to the floor laughing. What was with all this laughter, I couldn't hold back today, it was contagious; soon Sheri couldn't stop either.

"That striped number, I wouldn't be caught dead in, where did you get all these," I said touching the thin fabric, "I need something with some more, material." I said, holding it if front of me, looking in the bedroom mirror.

"Now come on, you are smaller than me, so on you there will be more fabric!" We settled on an animal print leather mini skirt with bra and matching panties, a dark brown push up halter went over the top. The shoes were the problem; we had to stuff the toes with toilet paper to fill them in so I would fit into the brown pumps. I looked down thinking how big my feet looked, my outfit looked okay, I liked the dress up role I was getting read to play, I felt like a sexy hooker, the colors matched my skin it was a good choice. My night attire fit like a glove and I wondered how Sheri, who was four or five inches taller, had fit into it. We picked a cute pink pleather outfit for Sheri that contrasted with her dark hair and olive skin; she looked like a super model, with me as her small sidekick.

After hours getting ready we prepared to enter into the fireplace room. I knew the reaction we would get before the door was pulled back. The men turned from the fireplace drinks in their hands, I watched as lust filled their eyes as they gave us the once over.

"Well this is a surprise, you both look great!" Dick said trying to sound calm, under control, and in charge, but it came across far from cool. Quinn shut his mouth that had just been hanging open. On his face was a grin that he quickly tried to hide.

"Dick, it shouldn't be a surprise," Sheri said as she strutted into the room, her high glass hooker heels clicking as she walked on the wood floors. I tried to follow standing up straight in the tall heals, maneuvering, but my main objective was to balance in the shoes and keep from toppling forward. I felt I looked like a baby doe taking her first steps as my legs tangled in the shoes.

"Now don't say anything Quinn or I will have to wrestle you to the floor," I said moving in front of him I did a spin, swaying my hips as I moved. I watched his brows rise and promptly go back in place. Dick walked over to the table and motioned us to all follow him. On the top was a bunch of electrical wire and equipment.

"We need you girls to be wired," Dick said moving to Sheri's pink pleather top and trying to figure out where to plant the listening device.

"We can't wear the bugs where they will be seen, we are going to have to take off most of our clothes once inside. The best place will be in our underpants," Sheri said

"How much clothes?" I asked, I was trying to act like it wasn't a big deal but my heart was racing with the thought.

I was a private person and the idea of being buck naked in front of people I didn't know made me pause.

"We will go down to our underwear and wrap a towel around us. You will do just fine," Sheri reassured me, "It's like wearing a bathing suit to the beach." I nodded and looked back at Dick.

"Lets get to it." Sheri unzipped her pink shirt and pushed it down on her hips revealing the top of her bright pink panties. "Put it inside of my panties." Dick picked up the device and I watched as his hand shook a little as he went down the front of her underwear, installing the small bug. He looked at me and I went over to stand in position, lowering my skirt as well, ready.

"Here I will do it," Quinn said as he took the silver bug from Dick's hand and proceeded to put his hand inside my panties. When it was in place, his hand lingered for a few extra seconds, I took a breath as his hand brushed against my pubic hair. I tried not to react because we had company, but the gleam in Quinn's eye told me that he had noticed my reaction and was pleased—MEN.

"Are we ready to go?" I moved to the door breaking the sexual tension that had started to rise in the room. Downstairs we found the girls in the living room. Ester had Amanda on her lap who was quite listening as she read to her. They got up and came over to join us at the door. Amanda jumped around Sheri.

"Sheri you look like my Barbie! I think I am going to call you Sheri Barbie!" We all watched as she skipped and hopped around Sheri singing "Sheri Barbie."

"Amanda, Amanda!" Ester called and she stopped to come and stand by her side. "That is not very nice." Amanda looked at Sheri.

"She does…look like my Barbie," Amanda whispered.

"It's okay, I like it, and you can call me that if you want." Amanda smiled up at Sheri. I took Ester's hand, trying to explain the outfits.

"We are going undercover," I whispered in her ear, her eyes lit up with excitement. "I will tell you all about it when we get back." Ester looked satisfied that she was being treated as an adult and walked us out the door and said "good-by."

We arrived at the Oasis Club in two cars followed by a black van with tinted windows. The men went in first; we waited twenty minutes and went to the door. The black van had moved to the back of the parking lot to a corner that was shadowed in darkness. Sheri took the lead and I watched as she pulled her club card out of her purse and presented it to the bald man at the door. Inside we went to the bar to get a drink, I couldn't remember the last time I had been to a bar and never to a special bar like this one specializing in sex. I was a little nervous, I slammed down a lemon drop martini and ordered a second, as I scanned the room for the men. They were at a table by the bar watching the dance floor, trying not to look at us. I watched Sheri examine the room and nod as she saw what she was looking for and wrote something on a napkin. She called the bartender and ordered Dick and Quinn drinks and sent the note to the table with the beers. I saw Dick read it and look at table five where an older gray—haired man with a pop belly sat eyeing the women around the room; he smoothed his hair and straightened his clothes as we watched.

A man with a great tan wearing an expensive suit entered the room and made his way to the bar looking from side to side seeing if anyone was watching him. He stopped short when he saw Sheri, I watched as she noticed him and gave a small nod and grabbed my hand and we made are way to the dance floor. Great I could feel the toilet paper in my shoes move around as we crossed the room, glad that Sheri had my arm. The sound of disco music filled the small space; bringing back childhood memories of my parent's house and a different time. I was lost in the loud noise of the speakers when Sheri's hand brought me back to reality. I looked and she had moved behind me and was rubbing her hand down the front of my halter top, grinding her hips into my backside. She was really good at role-playing, I better get with the program if this was going to work. I felt her breath on my neck.

"Loosen up, you can do it. The tan man's the target, smile at him." I pretended that I was a girl that liked girls and moved in rhythm against Sheri to the beat of the music. I reached behind and kissed her on the check and had to hold back a giggle. I looked doe eyed at the tan man, catching his gaze and not looking away as Sheri acted like she was bi. I was trying not to react but all of this rubbing and neck kissing was starting to turn me on. I was a girl that had never, never been interested in women and this reaction caught me by surprise, maybe I was just thinking those hands were Quinn's. The man approached us; I was soon sandwiched in the middle of him and Sheri, two taller people with little me being rubbed in-between. The smell of old spice and a shirt lived in all day greeted my nose as I looked at his conservative outfit, yet lusty eyes.

"Ladies would you like to join me in the back?" I looked at Sheri and she smiled at him and the three of us left the dance floor.

Quinn and Dick sat at the table not believing what they were watching. The girls' were the hottest in the room and every man couldn't turn away from watching them dance, they knew they were drawing attention.

When a man approached and started to touch them, it took all of Quinn's self-control to stay seated. He looked over and saw the same reaction on Dick's face. When the girls left with the man, they knew he was the target. Quinn and Dick waited ten minutes and moved to the back of the club towards the locker room, it was empty. Rapidly they changed into their towels leaving boxers on underneath and moved to the door blocked by the bouncer. There was a short line waiting to be allowed to enter the love den inside. Quinn rocked from side to side watching the line slowly move forward, at one point he almost went to the front and bust inside and Dick had put his hand on his arm to stop him. Quinn was not about to let Julie get trapped in a room with that man or any man as a matter of fact. Once they were inside Quinn hastily went down the dark halls looking from side to side for the girls. They were nowhere in sight, not caring, Quinn opened every door looking inside; many motioned him to enter and join in, admiring his large Viking golden chest and massive arms.

"Where are they?" Dick asked, starting to panic at the thought that they were in trouble.

"Call the van!" Quinn said as he went back down through the rooms searching one more time. Dick pulled out his phone and one of his men picked the phone up on the second ring.

"Have you guys seen the girls leave the club?" Dick asked.

"We have been trying to reach you. A few minutes ago the back door opened and both of them were ushered into a limo that is sitting in the back."

"Don't let that limo out of the parking lot! We are on our way!" Quinn and Dick moved to the back searching for the door to get out side, it was guarded with a huge black man that looked like a professional wrestler.

"We need to get out that door!" Dick said flashing his badge. The black man moved aside and went to open the door.

"A man and two women?" Quinn asked, "Is that all?"

"Yes Senator Shipfield and a tall dark-haired women and a small blond. They are in the limo."

"Thanks for your help" The men rushed outside, muscles popping, and adrenaline pumping, towels falling to the ground, to the limo that was gone.

******

The girls had followed the senator to the rear of the club. It was dark and they had to move fast down the long hallway to keep up. Behind a curtain was a large black man that nodded and opened the back door of the club allowing the three of them to exit. A long limo sat three feet from the back of the building, the door was open and I felt myself pushed into Sheri as we fell to the floor. For a moment nothing happened but as I pushed my way to a sitting position I felt some one hit the back of my head and I fell into darkness.

When I awoke I found that my hands where tied, my towel had slipped away, I went to pull it back in place and my hand couldn't move. I looked down I found that my underwear were in place, thank the heavens, a sharp pain hit me in the ribs; someone was moving right beside me. I felt a nudge and I tried to roll away from whomever it was, when I heard Sheri whisper, "Thank God you are awake!"

Calming down I turned around and found that she was also tied down, her eyes open, anger lucking in the corners. We both were on a large bed that was in a sunroom, I cold tell because it was a well-lit room with windows that allowed the suns rays to shine down on our bodies, it looked out into a large back yard full of mature trees. We could hear voices coming from the other room; someone was angry yelling at the top of his lungs.

"They have been at it for a while, I pretended to be knocked out when I saw that you where still down for the count. A man named Frank recognized you; I think He has seen your file. He has been telling the senator that they should dump everything and forget about Brazil, but it sounds like the senator is greedy and wants the project to continue. Here they come, play dead." Sheri said and we both closed our eyes and didn't move we had to buy time until we could be found.

A hand harshly grabbed my small chest, twisting the nipple. I cried out, the pain made my skin crawl, thinking who was touching me. Anger came to the surface. No one touched me that way and lived!

"See I told you she should be awake," the Frank man laughed, grabbing my breast again, enjoying the pain it caused me.

"You better remove your hand or I swear I will break it!" I yelled, the man snickered, letting out a lusty laugh; all I wanted to do was jam it down his throat. I watched as he moved over to Sheri and as he lifted his hand to touch her, the tan man shouted,

"Leave her, she is mine!"

"We have always shared the bitches, why is it different with this one?" Frank asked, not happy that he wouldn't get to taste this sexy woman.

"I checked her out, she has nothing to do with any of this and she came back to the club to find me because she was interested in me," the senator said, sure because of his large ego. "Isn't that right Sheila?"

I heard Sheri move on the bed, I watched as she looked into the senator's eyes smiling at him. Who was Sheila? He moved to the bed and untied her and she let him lift her into his arms, putting her long model arms around his neck pulling him closer.

Wow it must be great to be so good looking that men threw aside their common sense.

"I'm going to my room." The senator moved to leave and I watched Sheri whisper into his ear. He turned, "I think you are going to be out of luck tonight Frank."

"What are you talking about?" He slammed his fist on the bed making the mattress and me bounce in the air.

"My friend Sheila has requested that her new friend join us for the evening, she has never been with a women and would like her first time to be the three of us. Sorry about that." The senator smiled, looking forward to the night ahead.

"Oh no! What are you going to do when you are done with Redford?" Frank bellowed, moving toward the bed, blocking my view of the senator.

"You can have a go at her if you want when we are finished.

She is going to be shipped down to Brazil to the lab where we need to use her blood," the senator stated, not looking at Frank all his attention was on the dark beauty in his arms.

"I don't think that is a good idea, have you been able to get a hold of Smith? I thought we would take her to the island," Frank said, angry that this man would take all the ass for the night. He should not have helped him and should have stayed at the club where the company was way better.

"No, but he will call soon, he is taking care of the new shipment."

"What about our loose ends in Florida?" Frank said.

"It has already been taken care of. Now untie her! Bring her into my bedroom before you leave." The senator moved out the door, Sheri holding on to him, rubbing her mouth along his neck. He held her tight, acting like she was a delicate package.

I was untied and pushed forward, but before we got across the room, the Frank man reached around me and tried to put his hand down my underpants. I pushed his arm away and slammed him to the floor; he was on his back looking like a turtle that couldn't get up, his legs in the air. I was surprised that my strength was still working, strong as ever. I reached behind me and put my fingers around a heavy iron candleholder and smashed it down on top of his head. He laid still and I saw a small amount of blood that seeped out from under the thick gray hair. I moved around the room and in the kitchen pantry, I found packaging tape and I wrapped Frank's hands and feet just in case, using the tape to tie the large man to the heavy solid rock, living room table. If he woke up and got loose, it would take him a while. I remembered Sheri, seven to ten minutes had passed, and I hadn't heard any noise from the bedroom. I went in that direction and removed the mace out of the inside of one of my bra cups, this had turned out to be a sweet gift from Quinn.

Entering the bedroom, I found Sheri on the bed her bra had been removed and the senator's lips were latched onto a tit. Her eyes said, "Where have you been," as she ran her hands through the man's thick hair, faking a grown.

"I can't believe you guys didn't wait for me." The man turned his head, lust in his eyes as he continued to suck. I got on his back and put my legs around his waist my small arms went around his neck and I rolled him off Sheri. She saw the mace in my hand and took it out of my fingertips. When I turned my head, she sprayed the man in the eyes. He screamed, trying to get up off the bed to gain control of the situation. I held on as Sheri got off the bed and took the lamp off the nightstand and hit him over the head. He fell still.

"Grab the tape on the floor outside of the door!" I shouted, I continued to hold onto the man just in case he woke up, he was older than I had thought and I saw the glue that had held his perfect hair in place. We had him taped to a chair, by the time we heard the sounds of the sirens approaching in the distance. We both stood looking at each other feeling satisfaction about the job we had done.

"You okay?" I asked and Sheri understood I didn't mean physically.

"Yes, it wasn't that bad, you know I took one for the team, next time it is your turn," Sheri was happy that she could use what she had been given as a weapon. I was proud of her for being tough.

"Okay, this might be a lot more fun than working alone," I said, as the sound of the sirens had stopped; I knew everyone would be here soon. "Sheri you might want to put on your bra before everyone comes in."

"In all the excitement I forgot it wasn't on, thanks. That's all I need is for my new boss to see me this way. Do me a favor and not go into details about what happened in here," Sheri said, looking at me to see if I agreed.

"Don't worry, I understand, Quinn doesn't need to know everything, ethior," I handed her a towel and we both quickly wrapped them around our bodies. A few minutes later, the back door bust open, law enforcement officers, lead by Quinn and Dick entered the room. I could see the worry on Quinn's face, from across the room, he grinned when he saw I was safe. But it was funny to see his and Dick reaction of shock when they found Sheri and I wrapped in towels in the living room relaxing on the sofa having a bottle of expensive wine we had found in the senator's private stash. The bad guys knocked out at our feet covered in packaging tape.

"What took you guys so long?" We toasted our glasses and giggled at the look on the men's faces.

EPILOGUE

We all sat in the sitting room at Dick's family home; everyone seemed excited about the positive feedback that we had gotten from the White House after the assignment was over, but I know we all felt the letdown that you feel when a job is over. All of us would be parting ways soon and that sadness loomed over the room.

Quinn was going back to Brazil to tie up loose ends. He had asked me if I wanted to go with him, but I had told him no. I had my own things to take care of in the States. It was time for me to clean out my storage locker in Andover, Kansas and face what was in my parent's trunk.

Sheri was off to the Gulf of Florida to sell her house and move her things to Washington. She was going to rent the guesthouse in the backfield of Dick's family estate. He had told her that she didn't have to pay anything, but she wouldn't have it. She told him she would find somewhere else if he didn't let her pay. Nothing more had been mentioned again, I think he was just happy she would be near by were he could keep an eye on her.

Ester had inherited her father's wealth and a trust fund had been set up in her name. She would never have to work or worry about money. Dick had adopted her to keep her safe in the future, just in case anything ever leaked out about the cloning. She was to start ninth grade at a private school in the fall and was really excited to make new friends.

Senator Shipfield had been removed from his position for the penalty of redistributing the weapons research funds. As part of his agreeing to step down, all of what happened was kept out of the news. In exchange for a gag order, he couldn't say anything about the cloning or the drugs used on military officers, causing their deaths. Instead a statement was released implying he had used a prostitute service, taking the women across state lines breaking the law and had been asked to step down from his position.

Frank was barred from lobbying for any drugs for the next three years.

Smith had disappeared inside the long arms of military law and we weren't sure what had happened to him, we were not getting any information. We had heard that he could have been sent somewhere for reprogramming. I wasn't sure that I wanted to even know what that was or what the government did to fix someone like him. I thought of the top things I hated and made a mental note, never trust anyone that has been reprogrammed, unless they were your boy friend.

Dick cleared his voice and we all looked at him, tonight was our last night we would all be together and he had gone all out with lots of fancy food and wine.

"I have something to say." The room became quiet and I watched him move over to a bookcase and pull some papers from the top shelf. He handed the three of us each a large envelope.

"What is this?" I asked, feeling the heaviness of the package.

"Just look inside," Dick said, and we all dumped the contents onto our laps and started reading. Each of us had some orders and a pile of paper clipped money.

"You see ladies, you are being transferred to the CIA to work directly with me. So Julie you are going to have to get a place in

Washington too. All of you have an month to get your affairs in order and report back here in thirty days. Because the higher-ups liked the way this case turned out, I am being allowed to form a special team. The money is for you're past services and moving costs."

I was surprised and happy that we would be able to all work together, I had made some good friends and didn't want to lose that close feeling of family that I had recently acquired. I turned to look at Quinn, for some reason he wasn't smiling; he just sat there flipping back and forth through the papers.

"What is your problem?" I wanted to know. Was he not pleased that we would be in the same place and working together I wondered?

"A month is a long time to be away from you, maybe we could come back early and go out to that Oasis Club," he said, pulling a strand of my hair between his large fingers and leaning over to inhale the smell. It sent chills up my spine.

"Your so silly," I said, kissing him on the cheek, running my hand over his large arm feeling the bicep move as I touched it.

"You girls never told us the details of what happened in that house," Quinn said, Dick looked up this had caught his attention he watched Sheri and I, waiting for one of us to say something. Instead I had a question that I had forgot to ask Sheri.

"Sheri, by the way who was Sheila?" The men looked really puzzled.

"That is my sister's name, I used her ID's when I signed up at the club," she said.

"That was a good idea, it really saved us." I knew she was smart, but I wouldn't have thought of that. We smiled, remembering how we must have looked running around in our underwear.

We had a secret and I would never tell that's what agents did, didn't they? This was all new to the both of us, I was sure as time went by we would both get better at our job. The men sat waiting, as we skipped over their question.

"When you get back from Kansas why don't you plan on moving in to the guesthouse with me? It would be loads of fun," She watched me waiting for my answer. I thought it would be really cool to live with a friend; I had never had a roommate before.

Quinn was looking like it should be him asking me to move in but it would be better to take it slow. My mother had always said "a man never buys the cow if he can have the milk for free, or was that the meat." Whatever, he would be staying over when he was in town, but I would have my own space.

"Okay that would be great as long as you still don't want me to be your first!" I said laughing. I knew the men's ears would be perking up at that comment, that's why I had said it.

"What are you girls talking about? What did happen in that house?" Dick asked as he and Quinn gave each other a look and waited for the answer.

"A lady never tells," Sheri said and gave me a hug.

We looked at the men and laughed at the expressions on their faces. It was going to be a long month.

LaVergne, TN USA
10 February 2011
215886LV00004B/221/P

9 781451 271300